when
rivals *love*

BAYSHORE RIVALS BOOK THREE

USA Today Bestselling Author

J. L. BECK
C. HALLMAN

1

Slowly my eyes flutter open, but I can barely see anything. I'm immersed in darkness. It takes me a moment before I realize that I'm in the back seat of a moving car, my face sticking to the leather. The car takes a sharp turn, and my head lolls to the side. *Ugh.* It feels like my skull's been stuffed with cotton balls. My thoughts a blurred mess like I'm looking through a puddle of water that's mixed with mud, I can't figure out how I got here.

A wave of nausea overcomes me, my stomach churning like I'm on a roller coaster. I've never gotten car sick before, but right now, I could blow chunks. Slowly my thoughts return, and as I roll over on the seat, I'm reminded that someone put a cloth over my mouth... that someone drugged and kidnapped me.

Jackknifing in the seat, my vision blurs at the fast movement, and bile rises up my throat. Sucking air in through my nose, I get the nausea to fade away, and after a few more seconds pass, my vision fully clears, and I can make out the person in the driver's seat.

What the hell?

"Ber... ah, I mean... Milton? What the hell are you doing?"

His eyes find mine in the rearview mirror, "I'm really sorry, Harlow, but you weren't safe at the house, and it's my job to keep you safe." His eyes fall back to the road. There isn't an ounce of remorse or regret in his voice, and I have to wonder how sane he is right now.

Is this a joke? Some sick twisted bullshit my father is doing.

"So, you drugged and kidnapped me to keep me safe? Seems like the opposite if you ask me!" I try to keep my voice even, but patience escapes me, and it comes out as a yell.

"I'm sorry about the chloroform, but I needed to get you out of the house fast, and I knew you wouldn't have come with me willingly," he explains further.

He is right about that, I wouldn't have come with him because by leaving I'm endangering the people I love, but Milton doesn't know that, or if he does, he doesn't care. My gaze swings around the blacked-out SUV and then out the window. It's so dark, I can't make out where we're headed.

"Why do you think I wasn't safe at the house?"

"It's not that I *think* you're not safe. I know it."

"Explain, tell me, make me understand because right now you look more like the person trying to hurt me than anyone else."

With a loud exhale of breath, he starts to speak, "Remember at the rehearsal dinner when I bumped into the waitress, making her fall and your food went everywhere?"

"What the hell does a waitress tripping and dropping my food have to do with you kidnapping me?"

"It has to do with the fact that someone was trying to

poison you. I saw someone put something in your food as it was being brought out."

I blanch, the realization of what he's saying sinking heavily in my stomach.

Grasping at straws, I say, "Maybe you're wrong. Maybe you saw wrong?"

He shakes his head. "I'm not wrong, Harlow. I've been protecting you for a long time, and I've been doing this kind of work even longer. I'm trained in this kind of stuff, and I saw someone put something in your food. There is no wrong when you witness it with your own eyes."

Oh, god, maybe he isn't wrong. Maybe I am. Maybe someone is trying to kill me. It makes sense, the brothers told me someone was trying to hurt me, but I never wanted to believe it. Why would anyone want me dead?

"Why didn't you say anything? Why didn't you tell my father?" I yell while moving toward the door.

I'm scared and angry. I don't understand why someone would want to hurt me. After everything I discovered tonight about my father, and the Bishops, there is very little room left inside of me to deal with anything. I'm exhausted, both physically and mentally.

"Because I don't know if your father was involved or not. I need more information."

All of this is insane, completely insane. As badly as I dislike my father right now, I need to go to him, to tell him what happened, there is no way he could be involved, is there?

"You need to take me back right now," I order, but Milton continues driving like I didn't say anything at all. "I mean it, take me back!" I'm seconds away from kicking the back of his seat to get his attention.

"I can't, and I won't. I told you it's not safe."

Clutching a hand to my stomach, I feel the overwhelming need to vomit.

"Where are you taking me?"

"Somewhere that you will be safe." Great, that doesn't tell me anything. Folding my arms over my chest, I just sit there pouting like a teenager, because really, there is nothing else I can do. Not with the car going down the highway at sixty miles an hour.

I need him to stop so I can make a run for it. Deja vu settles in my mind, that was my plan the last time I got kidnapped. Didn't work out that great then, but what else can I do? It's not like I stand a chance fighting a man who is twice my size and works as a bodyguard, but I'm not going to let this happen without, at least, fighting back, the stakes are too high.

We drive on the two-lane highway for a while longer until Milton suddenly puts his turn signal on and switches lanes to take the exit. I perk up, my eyes catching on the rest stop sign in the beam of the headlights.

Keeping my lips firmly together, even though I have a ton to say, I wait for the car to stop. With enough adrenaline pumping through my veins, I reach for the handle just as the car comes to a stop. But all my plans change in an instant because before I even touch the handle, the door opens for me.

The cool night air rushes into the car. On instinct, I jerk back at the large dark figure that's magically appeared in front of me, blocking the exit.

A tiny squeak slips past my lips when he bends down and starts to climb into the back seat. *Oh, hell, no.*

Lifting my foot, I'm about to kick this bastard in the face

when my eyes catch on a familiar pair of chocolate brown ones. *Oliver.*

"Oliver..." I gasp as I lean back in the seat. I'm caught between wanting to hug him, and throat punch him all at once. When I see his trademark smirk that usually makes my insides tingle, anger wins out. All I'm feeling right now is simmering rage.

"Were you in on this?"

He had better not be, though, I'm certain he was.

"In on it? Baby, it was my idea," he chuckles.

Yup, definitely want to punch him now.

"You didn't actually think we were going to let you marry that asshat *Matt*, did you?"

"It's not your choice, and you don't know the danger you're putting all of us in by doing this... *again.*" My heart starts to break all over again. Every time I think I'm moving forward, learning to let go of the feelings I have for the Bishop brothers, one of them decides to reappear in my life.

"Drive," Oliver orders when he is in the car.

Milton throws the car into drive and pulls out into traffic. Oliver reaches for me, his fingers interlace with my own, and I can't bring myself to disconnect from him. I need his touch, need the warmth of his skin. It's like it gives me strength.

"We have evidence against your father. Leverage. You don't have to marry that prick to protect anyone. You aren't under your father's thumb anymore."

My face falls, my eyes move to where our fingers are joined. I don't understand how. I couldn't find any evidence, nothing to stop my father from hurting the Bishops. If I don't go back now...

"Stop thinking, I can see all the thoughts running

through your head. You're safe, we're safe, nothing is going to happen."

Looking up into his brown eyes, I ask, "How can you be sure?"

Even in the dark, I can feel his eyes burning a path over my skin.

"I thought you would be happy to get away from him," he whispers in defeat.

Moving closer to him, I lift a hand and force him to look at me. "I am, but I'm scared. I don't want my father to lash out at you or your brothers for this. I can't let anything happen to any of you."

"And we can't let anything happen to you either. Besides the whole scam marriage thing, you weren't safe there. Someone is trying to hurt you." The pain in his voice cuts through me like razor blades, and all I can think about is making him feel better. Crawling into his lap, I wrap my arms around his neck and bury my face into his neck. He immediately wraps his arms around me, crushing me to his chest. All I can hear is the heavy thump of his heart in my ear as it beats against his chest, his intoxicating scent filling my nostrils.

I spend the rest of the drive cradled in Oliver's arms, forgetting that Milton's in the car completely. I'm so content that the exhaustion wins out, and I don't even realize that I fall asleep until Oliver wakes me up with a gentle kiss to my forehead, we've pulled up in front of a hotel.

"We are here," he murmurs into my hair as I stretch my arms.

"Where is here?"

"We'll stay in this hotel, for now, there is security everywhere, and no one would expect us to be here. It's safe,"

Oliver promises. He takes my hand and helps me out of the car. We close the car door, and Milton drives off to who knows where. Right now, I'm too tired to care. Oliver leads me inside, and only then do I realize I'm wearing pajamas. Luckily, there is no one in the lobby when we pass through. I'm not sure what time it is, but it's still dark outside, so it must be very early in the morning.

We ride the elevator up to the ninth floor, the ding of the door opening wakes me up a tiny bit more, but by the time we are walking down the hallway to our room, I'm half asleep again. Oliver has an arm wrapped around my waist, and I'm leaning into his side, my legs are getting heavier with each step.

He stops and swipes a card through the door lock, making it click open. Together we enter the room, which looks more like an apartment. There is a large kitchen that opens up into a living room with a sitting area, huge TV, and even a fireplace.

"Wow, this is nice..."

My words are trail off when what I assume to be the bedroom door opens, and two familiar faces enter the room. Oliver releases me so Banks can pull me into his arms. He holds me tight for a few seconds, burying his face into my hair, breathing in my scent as I do the same with him. A calmness overtakes me, all the anxiety, fear, and sadness fading away.

He releases me and lets Sullivan have his turn. Sullivan circles my waist with his arms and hauls me up against his chest, giving me a bear-like hug.

"I missed you so much," he whispers against my hair, his breath tickling the fine hairs on my neck.

"You saw me yesterday," I giggle.

"That's too long, we need to see you every day," Sullivan replies thickly.

"Hey! I didn't see her yesterday, so move along…" Banks complains, grabbing my arm and pulling me away from Sullivan. "You look tired. Do you want to go to bed?"

The right thing to do would be to stay up and talk to them since I need to know what kind of evidence they have against my father, not to mention telling them about the things I found in my father's desk and what happened with Shelby in the office.

There are so many questions that need to be answered, so many things that need to be said, but all I can think of doing right now is closing my eyes and falling asleep.

Exhaustion is winning out, and after everything, I need some time to rest my brain.

Nodding my head, I admit, "I could go for a couple hours of sleep."

"Yeah, you look pretty tired," Sullivan says, admiring my face.

"Thanks," I say, laughing softly, "I have so much I want to talk about, but I'm dead tired. Like dead to the world."

"Sleep, then we can talk." Banks leads me into one of the bedrooms, and I fall on to the bed, the soft memory foam mattress swallowing me up as I sink deeply into the cloud-like material. A heavy blanket is pulled up to my chin, the weight of it against my body, making it hard for me to keep my eyes open.

I'm vaguely aware of Banks sliding into the bed next to me, and I sigh heavily when his arm snakes around my waist, and he pulls me back against his chest.

His warmth engulfs me, and with his steady breathing against my neck, I feel myself drifting off into the nothingness of sleep, wondering if when I wake up, this will all have been a dream.

Waking up the next morning, it takes me a few seconds to wrap my head around where I am. I'm in bed with not one but two of the brothers.

Banks still has his arm wrapped around me, his face buried into my neck. Oliver is lying on his side next to me, his brown eyes meet mine and hold my gaze.

"Were you watching me sleep?"

"Yes," he admits shamelessly. "It feels like it's been an eternity since I last saw you, and all I can think to do to make the ache hurt less is be near you."

I can't help myself. I reach for him and watch with anxious butterflies as he scoots closer until our faces are only an inch apart. I can feel his hot breath against my lips. I want to kiss him so badly it hurts, but the hunger flickering deep in his eyes tells me that it wouldn't stop with just a kiss, and we need to talk before we do anything else.

"What kind of evidence do you have against my father?"

"Milton recorded a meeting between your father and Xander Rossi, do you know who that is?"

"Yes," I admit, a small shudder runs through me at the memory. "I recently remembered overhearing a conversation between him and my dad years ago."

"Milton took a huge risk, but luckily your father never had a reason not to trust him."

"Why is Milton doing this? How did he even start working with you?"

"He actually came to us," Banks says sleepily from behind me.

"Sorry we woke you," I say, twisting my head around to meet his eyes.

"It's okay, I don't mind waking up as long as you are in my arms." Banks pulls me closer into him, and I can feel his hardened length pressing against my cheeks.

"So, Milton came to you?" I say a little flustered but trying to stay on subject.

"Yes, when you came back to Bayshore after your accident. He told us that he had been on your personal detail for a long time and that he couldn't stand how your parents treated you and lied to you."

"He disagreed even more with you marrying Matt," Oliver cuts in. "He didn't like how your family were pushing you into that marriage, and he knew Matt was an asshole with only his own gain in mind. So, he helped us keep you safe."

I suddenly feel horrible for not even calling him by his name for weeks. I was kind of a bitch to him when all he was trying to do was keep me safe, and not because my dad paid him to do so, but because he actually cared. I make a mental note to apologize for my behavior the next time I see him.

"So, what are we going to do now?" I ask curiously.

"It's up to you," Oliver says. "We have two choices. We can either go to the police with what we have, or we can use it as leverage to get your dad off your back."

I don't answer right away, I let both scenarios run through my head, both have huge risks, neither one is great. I'm not sure what's the right thing to do here, but I know one thing. Before I make a final decision, I need to talk to my father, I need to know about Phoebe and the connection between my father and George Bishop.

"Before I can even think about that, I need to tell you what I saw in my dad's office last night. I need to tell all three of you."

2

"Your dad and *Shelby*?" Sullivan asks, equal amounts of surprise and disgust lacing his voice.

"I don't know what I'm more shocked about. Shelby having an affair with your father or our dads being friends," Banks adds. "Even if it was a long time ago, I just can't wrap my head around it."

We are all sitting in the living room of the enormous hotel suite, and I just got done telling them about everything I saw last night. About my dad having an affair with my best friend, as well as the pictures and the love letter in the desk.

"Who do you think Phoebe is? You think she could really be your mother?" Oliver asks carefully.

"I don't know," I shrug. "I need to talk to my father."

"We got a burner phone, you can call him from it, but you can't tell him where you are or that we are with you. Not until we're sure that he is going to leave you alone," Banks warns as if I would do either thing.

"Got it." I reach out my hand, and Oliver places a phone

in it. When I look at the screen, I realize it already has a number pulled up. "Is that my dad's?"

When Banks nods, I hit the dial button and put in on speaker, so the guys can hear too. He answers after only two rings.

"Hello," his voice comes through the phone, and I can already tell he is aggravated by the deepness of his tone.

"Dad, it's me."

"Harlow, where in the world, are you? We have been worried sick. Are you with those Bishops again?"

"I saw you and Shelby last night," I cut my father's rant off, rendering him speechless for a few seconds.

"It's not what you think." My father tries to talk himself out of it.

"Hearing you fuck my best friend on your desk is pretty much confirmation, don't you think?"

"Jesus, Harlow," he says, sighing into the phone. "Okay, it is what you think, but I swear we never meant to hurt you, it just happened."

It just happened? I don't understand how that can just happen, but I don't think long on the matter. I don't care who my father fucks.

"Who is Phoebe?" My question seems to render him speechless once more. Proving to me just how important this Phoebe person is.

"How do you know that name?" he asks after a moment, his voice changing into a weird tone, almost nostalgic.

"I found the pictures and the letter in your desk," I explain.

"I can't do this over the phone, Harlow. Come home, and we'll talk. I'll explain everything to you." At my father's words, all three guys shake their heads no.

"I'm not coming home. Not today and maybe not ever again. Not after you tried to force me to marry someone for your own gain."

"I want you to marry Matt for your own good, not my own gains. Everything I've ever done was for you. Why is that so hard for you to understand or see?"

I roll my eyes so hard, I swear, I see my brain.

"It's hard to believe you when I know you're working with the mob. You are a criminal, and even worse, you made me into one too, when you had me plant drugs on Sullivan. Was that for my own good as well? Was it just training for a future job? For college?"

"We can't talk about any of this on the phone, Harlow. You need to meet me so I can explain everything. You don't know the whole story, and I'm not going to let you believe some lies that those Bishops are telling you."

"I have proof, you know. Proof that you are working with Xander Rossi."

"Harlow, listen to me. Do not get involved in this. Xander is not someone you want to mess with. If you have any involvement with him, anything against him, you need to destroy that proof right now."

"I'm sure you would like that."

"Harlow, this is not about me," my father's voice grows more frustrated. "I'm serious, you don't want to mess with Xander."

"I'm not destroying the evidence against you. I'm keeping it so you can't blackmail the Bishops or me ever again. I want to know more about Phoebe, but I'm not meeting you."

"Then I guess you will never get any answers—" The line goes dead, and for a moment, I just look at the phone in shock.

Did he just hang up on me?

Dumbfounded, I look up at the guys. "I need to go talk to hi—"

"No way," Oliver says before I can finish my sentence, his face stern and his arms crossed over his chest.

"I agree," Banks cuts in his eyes narrowing. "It's not safe."

My gaze swings to Sullivan, and I already know his answer is going to be no, as well. It's three against one here, but that doesn't mean I'm giving up. I need answers, all of them.

"What if you all come with me? Or Milton? Or everybody?"

"Your dad has a whole army of security, plus the mob behind him. The safest place for you is to be with us. We are not budging on this," Sullivan announces, and I can hear the promise in his statement. He's not going to change his mind.

"Fine..." I huff in defeat. "What about Shelby? Maybe I could talk to her and get some answers that way?"

"I guess we could see if she went back to Bayshore. As far as I know, she still has that job at the gallery. Maybe we can find her there or at class," Oliver suggests. "But if she isn't there, we are not going back to North Woods."

"Deal... let's go back to Bayshore." I stand up, ready to get moving when I realize all I have on is my pajamas.

"I don't have anything to wear."

"We'll get you some new clothes, but first..." Banks gets up, taking my hand, and with a mischievous smirk, he says, "We need to make up for lost time."

Sullivan and Oliver follow suit and stand.

"We need to show you just how much we missed you," Sullivan smiles, his voice deeper than normal, and the sound vibrates through me, awakening something deep inside me.

"And we did miss you a lot," Oliver says, and I suddenly feel like I'm burning up. The air around us changes like it's suddenly thicker. He extends his hand out to me, and I take it without hesitation.

"We don't have to do this. All three of us, I mean… If it's too much, you just have to tell us. We'll understand." I appreciate Banks trying to give me a way out, but he doesn't have to. I want all three of them, and I know they won't hurt me or test my limits. This isn't about just sex. It's deeper than that. This is about forging a connection that cannot be broken.

"Don't. This is what I want. To be with all three of you, together." I admit wholeheartedly.

"We want that too, but if you change your mind, you can tell us," Sullivan reminds me.

"I'll tell you if I do," I promise, and we all make our way to the bedroom. Once we reach the bed, Oliver and Banks start to strip me of my clothing. Their hands moving at breakneck speed. Once naked and bare to them, I watch each of them quickly strip out of their own clothing, my mouth watering in anticipation.

I've been with each of them, and with two of them at once but never all three, and while I'm only a little nervous about what's to come, there is an entire kaleidoscope of butterflies taking flight in my stomach. Warmth tingles low in my belly at the sight of the three of them shirtless—chiseled muscles that look like they could be carved from stone. As they climb up on the bed, no one says a word. Mainly because there are no words to be said.

Sullivan is the first to make a move, his hands gently cradle my cheeks as he comes in for a kiss. As soon as his lips meet mine, a fire sparks in my belly. I need him. I need all three of them. Out of the corner of my eye, I watch as Banks moves behind me, pressing hot mouthed kisses against my flesh.

I'm practically melting, and they haven't even reached the most important spots yet.

"I need to taste you..." Oliver all but growls, moving to his knees.

Breaking the kiss with Sullivan for half a second, I release a gasped, "Yes."

In a second, I'm moved to my back, all three of them hover over me with their eyes overlooking my body like I'm some kind of sacrificial lamb. Sullivan trails his hands down my body, while Oliver spreads my thighs. An electrical current ripples through me. It feels like I've been struck by lightning.

Banks leans forward his hot breath fanning against my hardened nipple. The look in his eyes screams hunger. He wants to devour me from the inside out. And I'll let him. I'll let him and his brothers do whatever they want to me.

"Oh, god..." The words just fall from my mouth when Banks' lips circle my nipple, and Oliver licks me from ass to slit.

"Fuck," Sullivan exhales, licking his lips one last time before they crash against my own. Oliver worships me with his tongue, feasting on me like I'm his last supper. Banks alternates between each breast flicking furiously against the tight nub before slowing down, teasing me at a treacherous pace.

While Sullivan may seem as if he's doing nothing, he is kissing me like a woman should be kissed, with love and adoration. I moan between our kisses, feeling my pulse pound in my ears, and my body shudders as red hot heat spreads through my limbs.

"Do you have any idea how pretty you are when you're coming?" Sullivan whispers into the shell of my ear as he peppers kisses along my throat. "Your pale cheeks are tinted the color of roses, and your chest rises and falls so rapidly. I've never seen your eyes so big and bright. Fall apart, sweetheart, and I promise, we'll catch you."

I'd never before thought that the cliché come on command thing worked, but it's like my body is tethered to his words, waiting with bated breath for his next command. Colorful spots of light appear before my eyes as they drift closed, my entire body shaking, a whole array of fireworks going off inside my belly.

"Fuck," Banks exhales, "holy shit..."

Oliver continues to feast on me, even as I drift down from my orgasm like a feather floating in the wind. From that moment on, I'm melting, becoming a goopy mess of soul-searing post-orgasmic bliss.

I can feel the sheets growing wet beneath my ass. I'm soaked, lying in a puddle of my own arousal. I should be embarrassed by how wet I am, but that's the last thing on my mind. My hands move to his hair, and I hold him in place between my thighs, needing him and the pleasure he gives me like it's my next breath.

Oliver spreads me with his fingers and licks my clit with an unbridled hunger. I feel the tingling build deep inside my core again, my back slightly arching off the bed, when Oliver's fingers move down to my other opening. Before I can think about how wrong this is, his finger is massaging me there, and all that's left in my mind is how good it feels.

"You like that?" Banks asks, his voice low and husky.

"Yes," I admit in between heavy panting. My moans become even louder when Oliver pushes the tip of his finger inside, probing the tight ring of muscle while simultaneously working my clit with his tongue. Banks and Sullivan have their hands on me too, I have lost track of who is touching me where. All I know is that I feel like I'm being worshiped by these men.

When Oliver dips his finger into my ass even further, while sucking on my clit for all he's worth, I'm tipped over the edge once more. I go off like a rocket, soaring through the air, shattering into a million little pieces in the night sky. Tremors wrack my body post-orgasm, and I whimper like a wounded animal as Oliver releases his hold on my thighs.

He climbs up the king-size bed and lies down next to me, he turns my head so I can see him. I'm still coming down from the second orgasm, my limbs feel heavy and featherlight all at once.

"I want you to ride me, baby, and while you do that, Banks is going to claim your ass," Oliver orders, beckoning me with his finger to come to him.

None of the brothers speak as I crawl on top of Oliver, who is obviously leading the show tonight.

"What about Sullivan?" I groan as he fills me up with his thickness. It's so hard to think about anything but the burning fire that snakes up my spine as he bottoms out inside of me.

A mischievous grin appears on Oliver's full lips. "Don't worry about him, sweetheart. He'll be coming down your pretty throat while you fall apart over and over again."

My chest expands and fills with oxygen, but it doesn't

feel like I'm actually breathing. In fact, none of this feels real at all. Them, me, us being together like this.

Oliver reaches up and cradles my cheek gently, his touch drawing me from my rampant thoughts. "Is that okay? Is this what you want?"

Nodding my head, I watch as the brothers arrange themselves on the bed. Banks coming up behind me, his cock pressing against my ass, and Sullivan moving to just above Oliver's head. Saliva pools in my mouth as my eyes catch sight of Sullivan's thick cock bobbing in the air. I want it. I need it.

Air swooshes from my lungs as Oliver enters me deeply, at a new angle, the head of his cock brushing against the back of my channel. I lean forward and wrap my hand around Sullivan's cock, my insides tingling with pleasure as he releases a hiss through his teeth.

"Fuck, if your mouth feels anything like your hand, I'm done for." Smiling, I stroke his dick up and down while the pleasure in my own core burns hotter and hotter.

Oliver lifts one of his hands, keeping the other firmly in place on my hip, and plucks at my overly stimulated nipples, and then I feel it... something warm and sticky sliding down my ass crack. Banks' fingers move through the unknown liquid, and I shudder as he reaches my puckered asshole, his thumb pressing against the tight muscles of my hole.

"Relax, baby, I won't take this virgin hole until you're ready. Till you're spent, nothing but a withering mess." His thumb presses against the tightness, and without thinking, I push back against him, wanting him there.

My ass pulses and, even though, there is pressure, and a tinge of pain, it lessens as Oliver strokes me deeply with his cock. Banks moves his finger in and out gradually, so slowly that I almost forget that he's there.

The grip I have on Sullivan's cock tightens, and I lean forward, bringing my lips to the smooth head. He groans as I wrap my lips around him and drag my tongue on the underside. A drop of salty warm liquid hits my tongue, and there is something so erotic about that, I can't help but moan around his length.

With Sullivan in my mouth, Oliver in my pussy, and Banks playing with my ass, my whole body is on fire. My senses are overwhelmed, and my brain is flooded with endorphins, making it impossible to think about anything besides what I am feeling right this moment. And what I'm feeling is every nerve ending in me being charged and ready to burst, sending me into oblivion.

Banks adds a second finger, stretching my tight hole just as Oliver picks up speed. Sullivan is also growing more eager. His large hands cupping my head, holding me in place as he thrusts into my mouth, his hard length sliding in and out over my tongue until he hits the back of my throat and I gag a little.

I didn't think I could possibly come again since I'd already come twice, but somehow, I am already teetering on the edge again. I'm consumed with need for them. My body screaming for their touch. My mind is on the verge of insanity. I feel like I imagine a drug addict must when they're trying to get their next fix. Oliver, Banks, and Sullivan are my drug, a fix I crave more than anything else.

Overwhelmed with need, I suck Sullivan as hard as I can, wanting him to come, wanting to give him pleasure like he gives me. He growls like some kind of animal while his cock swells in my mouth, his fingers twist in my hair, pulling on some strands. I don't know what it is about that small pain on my scalp, but it sends me over the edge. Pain and pleasure mixing together, creating a beautiful symphony of pleasure. I come hard, moaning around Sullivan, and like a chain reaction, he comes apart as well. Salty warm seed fills my throat as ecstasy ripples through me.

Oliver's fingers are digging into my hips as he buries himself so deeply inside of me, I can feel him in my belly. Banks pushes two of his fingers inside my ass deeper than before, the foreign feeling only prolonging my orgasm.

My vision goes blank, and my body goes limp as I come down from my third climax. Sullivan slips out of my mouth slowly, leaving a salty train of cum behind on my tongue. He still cradles my head when he kisses me softly before climbing off the bed. As soon as he disappears, I collapse on top of Oliver.

"I think you are relaxed enough now," Banks announces, chuckling behind me. "Are you ready for me, baby?" He runs his hand over my ass, and up my lower back, his simple touch feels so intense.

"Yes..." I half moan.

Banks removes his fingers and replaces it with the smooth head of his cock. He pushes against the tight ring, and all I can feel is pressure. His cock is much bigger than his fingers, and for a moment, I don't think it's going to fit.

"Relax," Oliver whispers in my hair and thrusts inside me, rubbing against my clit as he does. The sensation relaxes me more than his words, and I loosen up enough for Banks to slip inside of my ass.

"There you go," Banks growls, his voice strained like he is trying to hold back. Slowly, he inches his way inside of me while Oliver momentarily stills. "How does that feel?"

"I feel... full, so full..." My voice comes out breathy, just like my whole body feels right now. "But it feels good... so good."

At my words, Banks starts moving a little more, and a small whimper escapes my lips.

"Are you sure?" Oliver asks, running his hands over my arms and shoulders.

"Yes, I want you to move. Both of you," I urge, and they don't need another invitation. Oliver starts moving, thrusting again, and Banks starts to match Oliver's pace. The feeling is new and almost too much, but I don't want it to stop.

"Fuck, Harlow," Banks groans behind me as they fall into a rhythm. "You don't know how good this feels..."

"I'm not going to last long like this," Oliver says, his voice strained like he is barely holding on.

"Me neither, I'm about to come," Banks growls, and shortly after, I can feel him growing even bigger inside of me, his movements growing frantic, and his hand landing flat between my shoulder blades, pushing me down on to Oliver's chest. I bury my face into the crook of his neck. Oliver tries to match his brother's strokes. Both of them thrusting inside of me furiously now, and all I can do is lie there and take the enormous amount of pleasure they're giving me.

They come almost simultaneously. Oliver holding me close to him, and Banks leaning over my back, kissing my shoulders until he stills inside of me.

I've never felt so spent in my life. I'm physically drained but emotionally full. This was so much more than sex; it was us becoming one. Four people coming together and proving how much they belong as one.

"I love you," I murmur into Oliver's skin.

"I love you too," Oliver replies.

"You have no idea how much I love you," Banks says in between kisses to my heated skin.

"I love you too, Harlow, we all do." Sullivan appears next to the bed. I turn my head to look at him. "I ran a bath for you. It's ready when you are," he smiles, and all I can think of is how I got so lucky?

3

*I*t's weird to be back in Bayshore, maybe because I didn't think I would ever return here. It all looks the same, like the college town I remembered it to be. With bars, coffee shops, bookstores, and small 24-hour convenient stores on every corner; to fill every student's needs.

"We're going to drop you off at the gallery, but we won't leave you there alone. We'll be right outside in the car," Oliver explains as if we are planning some kind of super-secret mission.

"I'll be fine. It's an art gallery, and it's not like anybody would expect me to be here. I'm just going to walk in and see if Shelby is here so I can talk to her. If she isn't, I'll walk right back out, and we'll think of another plan, okay?" I look between the guys and wait for all three to give me a small nod before I open the door and get out of the car.

I can feel their eyes on me as I walk down the sidewalk toward the storefront of the gallery. A pounding forms behind my eyes and the sense of deja vu overcomes me. I continue walking until I'm in front of the glass door, my hand on the handle ready to pull the door open when the memory rushes in like water flooding a basement, seeping in through all the open cracks.

"I'm looking for Shelby. I'm sorry to show up here, I know she is working but this is kind of an emergency."

"Who?" *The woman looks genuinely confused, her eyebrows drawing together.*

"Shelby," *I say louder, she must have not heard me clearly.*

"Doesn't ring a bell. Is she one of our artists?"

"Oh...ah, maybe... maybe I'm at the wrong gallery, I'm sorry," *I say embarrassed, before turning on my heels.*

"This is the only gallery in town, miss."

I freeze with my hand hovering inches away from the doorknob. My mind goes blank and then this feeling of utter dread creeps its way up my spine and settles into the base of my skull.

Nothing makes sense, everything I thought I knew is wrong. My life built with building blocks of lies and deceit and like a Jenga tower someone pulled the one piece that has it all crashing down.

I feel like I'm trapped in this moment, my mind frozen in time. My thoughts hovering somewhere in between disbelief and unbelievable despair.

"Are you okay, miss?"

When I shake out of the memory, I'm not sure how long I've been standing there, but it feels like an eternity. I don't know why I'm so surprised by this lie. I already knew she was lying to me about numerous things, so why does this feel even worse?

"Harlow? What's wrong?" Banks comes out of nowhere, his hand coming to rest on my lower back.

"She never worked here," I answer. "I just remembered it. She lied to me about this too."

"I'm sorry... come on, let's get you home," Banks coaxes, his voice laced with concern. I let him lead me down the sidewalk, my mind still reeling from the recovered memory.

For some reason, I can't shake the feeling that there is more... more to this story... more I need to remember. It isn't until we are about to cross the road that it hits me. The most important memory of all. The final piece to the puzzle...

I look up, the scenery changing around me, the ground beneath me suddenly seems different. Sounds piercing through the fog surrounding my brain. Someone is screaming, but I can't make out what is being said. Then something catches my eye. I look up to see two bright lights heading straight for me. But I'm not fast enough, there is no time.

I watch in shock as the engine revs up, the car coming at me, and all I can do is stand there like a deer caught in the headlights... literally.

There is a moment, just before the impact, where the headlights are so close that they don't blind me, I can look above them, see through the windshield and get a look at the person who is trying to kill me.

It's only for a split second that I see her eyes; cold and detached, full of hate, and I don't understand why? Why does she hate me that much? Why would Shelby try to kill me?

"Harlow?" Banks is suddenly right in front of me, his hands on my shoulders, shaking me gently as if he is trying to wake me up from some nightmare. But I'm not asleep, this is not a dream, this is reality. Shelby, the person I thought of as my best friend my entire life, hates me, hates me so much that she wants me dead. My chest heaves, and it feels like a piece of my heart is breaking off.

Why? Why would she want me dead? Did I do something that I don't remember?

"Harlow? Harlow! You're freaking me out. Please tell me what's wrong," Banks questions frantically. I can see him, but not really. It's like I'm lost in my thoughts, trying to thread them back together.

"It was Shelby... I... I remember. Shelby was the one that tried to kill me. She hit me with the car on purpose. I saw her, it was her," I continue rambling on more to myself as Banks leads me to the car, halfway carrying me at one point.

He helps me into the back seat and buckles me up. Oliver and Sullivan twist around in the front seat their faces conveying a similar concern to Banks.

"What happened?" Oliver asks, but I can't say the words out loud again, they hurt too much.

"Just find a hotel. I'll explain everything there. We need to take care of Harlow first. She's remembering things," Banks explains, and Oliver takes that as his cue to drive off, pulling into city traffic with ease, leaving the gallery and the memories behind us, but not forgotten. *Why? Why would she do that?*

Banks slides across the bench seat and closer to me until his body is practically against mine, his body heat seeps into every pore of my body, soothing me in an instant like a blanket wrapping around me on a cold winter night.

Unable to resist, I turn to him, seeking the comfort he gives, burying my face into his chest. Without realizing it, I start to sob, letting all the anger, frustration, confusion, and hurt out. The tears fall from my eyes rapidly, and I don't even attempt to wipe them away.

By the time we get to the hotel, my vision is blurry, and there is a throbbing pressure inside my skull that seems to expand with each second. Oliver goes inside to check us in so that when we get out of the car, we can go straight to the room.

When we make it up to the room, Banks leads me over to the sectional, and the guys circle around me. All I can do is stare down at my hands, the same thoughts circulating in my mind.

"Why? Why would she want me dead? Why would she do something like that? We were supposed to be friends. She was my best friend, and…" I continue to mumble beneath my breath like a crazed person.

I can feel the brothers' eyes on me, and when I look up, I see nothing but anguish and worry flickering in their gazes.

"Shhh, baby, it's okay." Oliver soothes this time. What would I do if I didn't have them right now? If I was stuck back in my father's mansion? Shelby could easily get to me there. Then it hits me.

"I could've died. She could've killed me and gotten away with it, and no one would have known." The weight of that knowledge feels like an elephant sitting on my chest.

"If it was Shelby who hit you with the car at the art gallery, then I'll bet anything that she was the one to push you off the boat the night you almost drowned." Banks says.

"I can't believe this. I didn't particularly like Shelby, but I honestly didn't think she would be capable of something like this. I don't hit women, but I really want to hurt her for doing what she did to you," Sullivan hisses as if he's in pain.

"I just want to know why? What did she have to gain from killing me?" The tears start to fall again, and I don't understand why I'm crying over her. She doesn't deserve my tears.

"No one knows, but you can bet we'll figure it out. From here on out, it's us versus everyone else. We're not trusting anyone outside this room. No one is going to take you away from us or hurt you again."

Opening my mouth to say something, the words disappear, sticking to the roof of my mouth like peanut butter, and then I realize it wasn't words I needed to expel. I feel my stomach churning like I've just been on the longest roller coaster of all time. In a second, I'm flying from the sectional and heading for the nearest door.

Oh, god. I'm not going to make it.

I don't even get halfway to the bathroom before vomit erupts from my throat, splattering across the pristine floor. I empty the entire contents of my stomach while someone holds back my hair and someone else rubs soothing circles over my lower back. I don't look back to see who it is, mostly because I'm too embarrassed to look at anyone right now.

When my body is done convulsing, my throat burns, my eyes tear up, and my head throbs in pain. I feel disgusted and ashamed when I straighten back up to see all the guys standing around me while there is a puddle of vomit in front of me.

"I'm sorry…"

"Don't be ridiculous and apologize for being sick," Sullivan tells me. "Come on, we'll get you cleaned up." He gently takes my arm and pulls me toward the bathroom.

"I should clean this up," I complain, trying to pull my arm away.

"I'll call room service. Don't worry about anything, just go take a bath," Oliver waves me off, and Banks falls in step with Sullivan and I. Flanking me on both sides, they take me to the large master bathroom. Banks turns on the water, filling up the large garden tub while Sullivan starts to take off my clothes he just bought me this morning.

"I don't know what happened. I was fine one minute, and then I wasn't."

"It's okay, that was a lot to take in. I don't know if I could have stomached all of this either. Seriously, don't feel bad because there is nothing to feel bad about," Sullivan soothes, trying to calm me down.

When I'm completely naked, Sullivan takes my hand and helps me to get into the now half-filled tub. The water is the perfect temperature, and I sink into the bubbly goodness with a sigh. It feels like I'm sinking into a bath of heaven. Banks gets two washcloths, handing Sullivan one. They each squirt some soap on to their cloth and start washing me with it. Sullivan starts at my feet while Banks starts at my shoulders.

Closing my eyes, I let them massage and clean every inch of my flesh. Their hands move over my skin, and as if there is some kind of magic involved, all the tension and worry evaporates into thin air.

In this space, no bad feelings or worry can get to me. Nothing can touch me right now. By the end of my bath, my body is so relaxed, I feel boneless, my muscles have turned to jelly sometime in the last thirty minutes, and now I can barely keep my eyes open.

"You ready to come out?"

"Yeah," I barely nod.

Banks offers me his hand and helps me out of the bath while Sullivan grabs a bathrobe, holding it open for me. My arms slide into the fluffy fabric one at a time, and Sullivan closes the belt around my waist, tying me up like a perfectly wrapped gift.

"I like this," I giggle. "You guys taking care of me. It makes me feel like a princess. Like I'm important."

"You better get used to it," Banks tells me, right before he surprises me by picking me up bridal style. Letting out a startled squeal, I throw my arms around his neck. "'Cause we're not planning on stopping any time soon."

He carries me out of the bathroom, and the strong citrus odor of cleaning solution tickles my nostrils. Room service must have already come and cleaned up the mess I made earlier.

Banks places me on the bed, and as if on cue, Oliver walks in, holding a tray of food and puts it on the bedside table, I look at it wearily. Crackers, an assortment of prepared fruit, hot tea, and ice water sit before me. None of it looks all that appetizing, but then again, I did just barf all over the floor.

"I had them bring up stuff that I know will ease an upset stomach," Oliver explains as if he can read my mind. I don't know what to say, so I just push from the bed a little and wrap my arms around his middle. Oliver bends down and returns the hug.

"Thank you, no one has ever taken care of me the way that you all do."

"Stop saying thank you. We do it because we want to, not because we're obligated to.

"We love you, Harlow, and nothing has, or ever will change that. Not our parents. Not yours. Nothing. The circumstances of our relationship might not be perfect, or even common, but that doesn't make what we all have any less special." Banks intercepts, and my heart swells, growing bigger with each beat.

Tears well in my eyes. I'm consumed by them. My heart beats for them each in its own way. There is no me without them.

"We're supposed to hate each other, but it seems all we've ever done is love each other."

"Because we weren't meant to. Before, we just let our parents dictate our lives, but that won't happen again."

"Good, because I don't know what's going to happen next," I admit while nibbling on one of the crackers. Not only do I feel like crap, but I truly have no idea where to go from here. Do I stay hiding out with the Bishops for eternity? Not that I wouldn't like that, but it's not really all that feasible of an option.

Out of the corner of my eye, I see Banks rubbing at his chin. He looks to be lost in thought, and I wonder what he's thinking about. Each brother is handsome beyond measure, how the hell did I end up with all three of them?

Sullivan clears his throat, drawing all the attention in the room to him.

"You said our father was in the photos you found in your father's desk. The one with the mystery woman... Phoebe?"

Swinging my gaze to him, I stare in confusion. "Yes. Your father was in some of the photos. I had planned to ask my dad more about it, but as you know, he hung up on me before I had the chance. He won't talk to me again until I go back to North Woods, and none of you will allow that."

"Because your father is crazy," Banks chimes in.

"Because Shelby is still out there walking free," Oliver adds another brick of worry on their ever-growing pile. "We need to tell the police, Harlow. Are you up for that?"

All of their concerns weigh heavily on me, weighing down my heart. I don't take them lightly because I see how much I mean to them now and how dangerous things really are, but I didn't escape one ivory tower just to be trapped in another.

"Yes," I sigh. "I'll call them, but I still want to talk to my father. Staring down at the comforter, I say, "I understand why you don't want me to see him right now, and I'm okay with that, but I'm not some fragile piece of glass. I don't just want answers... I need them, which means eventually I won't have an option but to see my father again." Silence blankets the room, and I peek up through my lashes to see if they've disappeared into thin air.

Nope, they're still inside the room, and currently staring holes through my flesh.

"I have an idea." Oliver is the first to break the silence.

"Well, what is it?" Banks asks impatiently.

"We could bring you to our father..." His voice trails off, and I wonder if he's being serious or not.

"Your father would let you bring me to your house?" I ask, trying to hide the surprise from my voice.

Sullivan shrugs, "What's the worst he could do? Tell us to leave? We can't let you near your father right now, so the next best thing would be our father."

"Maybe he can piece the missing pieces of your puzzle together?" Oliver adds.

"Or he could be a huge prick and make things ten times worse," Banks mutters under his breath. Oliver and Sullivan look at him, their features hardening.

"You aren't helping."

Banks lifts his hands as if to say he's innocent. "Look, I'm not trying to be a negative nelly here. I want Harlow to get all the answers she needs just as much as you both do, but Dad isn't going to take well to us bringing a Lockwood home." Our gazes meet as he says the next words, "Last names don't mean shit to us, but Dad still sees her as the enemy, and I don't want her caught in his crosshairs."

To many, I might be weak, but I am mighty, and if I want answers, I may have to cross bridges that shouldn't be crossed. I may have to do things that I shouldn't do, but I'll do what I need to do. No one is going to dictate what happens in my life anymore.

"Let's do it."

"Seriously?" Banks runs a hand through his hair as if he's agitated. Was he not expecting me to go along with this?

"Yes, I want answers. Your dad has some. Let's do it. What's the worst that could happen?"

"'Kay, I'll make the arrangements, and tomorrow we'll visit our parents," Oliver announces as if it's final to his brothers.

Banks leaves the room a moment later, and Sullivan walks over to the bed and crawls into the vacant spot left beside me.

"Is he going to be okay? I ask. I kind of want to chase after him but know he needs the space.

"He'll be fine. He's just worried about what our dad will say or try to do to you."

I nod, understanding completely.

"Our father won't touch you. Not if he wants to live." Oliver's words have a sharp edge to them, and I shiver wondering if he really means that. Would he, and his brothers go against their parents for me? Would they risk it all for me?

I guess we'll find out.

Oliver gets out his phone and hands it to me. "Now to the hard part. You need to call the detective investigating your hit and run case and tell him what you know."

Looking down at his phone, I realize the detective's

number is already pulled up. "How do you have his number?"

"We had to make sure they knew the whole story and were doing their jobs. We regularly talked to the detective and checked in to see if there were any updates."

"Oh." I probably shouldn't be surprised by that, but somehow, I still am. I just can't get over how committed they are to me. Even when I didn't even know who they were, they took care of me, watched out for me.

Hitting the green call button, I hold the phone to my ear and wait for someone to answer while trying not to think about what I'm about to do. The person I thought was my best friend really isn't, and I'm about to send her to jail... maybe for a very long time.

4

The drive to the Bishop estate isn't that long, but it seems like an eternity when you're as nauseated as I am.

"Are you sure you're okay?" Sullivan asks, his forehead scrunched up in concern.

"Yeah, I'm good. Like you said, it's just a little hard to stomach all of this. All these emotions, all these questions surrounding my life, it's really weighing on me. Hopefully, your dad can clear up at least some of the confusion."

Banks grunts next to me, his gaze fixed on something outside the window. He's barely spoken since we decided to come here. I know he is unhappy with it, but I can't think of another way to actually figure out what's going on, at least not one that doesn't involve going back to my father. I need some answers, and right now, George Bishop is my best bet.

Reaching across the back seat for Banks, I latch on to one of his wrists and pull him closer. I half expect him to pull away and tell me, no, but he lets me interlace my fingers with his without complaint. When he finally turns his head, his sea-blue eyes find mine, and the worry swimming in their depths crashes into me like a tidal wave.

"We're going to be okay," I assure him. It sounds like a promise, and even though I have no way of actually keeping the promise, I don't mind saying it this way. Maybe because I will do whatever I can, whatever it takes, to make it happen. We have endured too much heartache to not get our happily ever after.

He gives me a halfhearted smile and a slight nod. I wish I could do more, take his worry away. Take all of our worries away, but I can't.

"We're almost there," Oliver says from the driver's seat, and Banks stiffens next to me. I squeeze his hand, hoping to calm him down, but the closer we get to the house, the more on edge he seems. His body goes rigid, tightening like a rubber band that's being pulled tighter and tighter.

"You sure it's a good idea to just show up without calling first?"

"We're their kids, we don't have to announce our visit," Sullivan tells me.

"Yeah, but you usually don't bring me along."

A few minutes later, we pull up to a large brick suburban home that looks a little bit like a small castle. It's beautiful, and I can't help but stare at it. It's gorgeous with high walls, and perfectly sculpted hedges. If it looks like this on the outside, I can't imagine what it looks like on the inside.

"Wow, that's your house?" I ask while continuing to gawk at the building.

"My mom likes to pretend she's a queen," Sullivan says, throwing me a wink.

We get out of the car and start walking toward the front door. Suddenly the reality of being here hits me, and I start to get really nervous. Looking over my shoulder, I catch Banks watching me. His gaze softens, and he extends a hand out to me. I gladly take it, letting his touch calm the storm inside of me.

"Don't worry, we won't let anything happen to you, and if my dad dares to talk down to you, we'll be out the door," Banks soothes me. Our roles reversed now.

Oliver and Sullivan walk ahead of us. Opening the front door with a key, we all walk into the house, which opens to a large grand foyer that matches the outside of the house. A gigantic, fancy chandelier hangs in the center of the entrance, a rounded staircase leading to the upper level, worthy of a queen to walk down.

"Mom... Dad..." Oliver calls loud enough that everybody in the house should here, even considering the size of it. A moment later, the sound of high-heeled shoes against the tile floor echoes through the foyer.

"Oliver?" A shrill voice fills the space a moment before a petite blonde woman appears in the doorway. "Boys..." Her tone is upbeat, excited to see her sons, she smiles widely. That is until she sees me standing behind Oliver and Sullivan.

Her smile falls and is quickly replaced with a frown. That frown deepening further when she looks between Banks and me and sees that we are holding hands.

"Hey, Mom," Sullivan greets, walking toward her and giving her a kiss on the cheek. She grabs on to his arms, holding him to her and whispers something in his ear. I can't hear from where I stand, but I can imagine she is asking him what the hell I'm doing here.

Sullivan straightens up, refusing to whisper, he says out loud. "We were hoping to talk to Dad and ask him some questions about the time when he and Harlow's dad used to be friends with Phoebe."

I can practically see the blood drain from Chloe Bishop's face, her eyes go wide, and she takes a step back as if she is trying to get away from the situation.

"How... how do you know... about that?" She stumbles over her words, looking uncomfortable and wary.

"From Harlow's dad. Well, he didn't tell us, but Harlow found some pictures and some letters in his desk," Oliver explains.

"I see," she says, and as if she remembers to compose herself, she perks up. A fake smile spreads across her face. "Well, come on in boys... and *Harlow*." Banks' grip around my hand tightens at the way she says my name, but I give him a look that silently tells him it's okay. I can hold my own. I won't let anyone hurt the men I love or me, for that matter.

She waves us inside, and we follow her through the house like little sheep.

"Your father is in his office working, but I'm sure he can make time for you," she chimes, her voice high-pitched and strained somehow. She is obviously nervous about taking us to her husband. The tension between all of us grows thicker. I have to force air into my lungs now. It's getting harder to breathe.

When we get to a large set of double doors, she stops and looks back at us one more time, as if she's waiting for somebody to say something. Maybe she's hoping we'll tell her *just kidding* or something like that. When no one says anything, she lifts her hand and knocks on the door lightly.

"Yes, come in," A muffled male voice carries through the closed door.

Mrs. Bishop opens the door and walks in hesitantly, all of

us following closely behind her. George Bishop sits behind his desk, holding a phone to his ear, scribbling something down on a piece of paper. His eyes are trained on whatever is in front of him. I now see where his sons get their looks from. Even though he is as old as my father, he still manages to look young and fit.

"Okay, and what's their counteroffer?" he says to the other person on the phone. He looks up, his face an unreadable mask. The pen which was dancing over the paper a minute ago stills in his hand as he takes us in. "I'm gonna call you back."

Mr. Bishop hangs up the phone and sits the device on the table next to him.

"Chloe... Kids... what's this all about? he asks carefully.

"Who is Phoebe?" I blurt out my most pressing question.

George's eyes find mine, and I'm surprised by the way he looks at me. I was expecting animosity, resentment, maybe even hate. Instead, all I find is sadness and reminiscence. Almost like I'm an old friend he hasn't seen in years, and he is sad about the fact that it's been so long.

"Chloe, dear, do you mind leaving us to talk for a while," he asks his wife, who seemingly is more than happy to have the opportunity to get out of here.

"Of course, I'll be in the kitchen preparing dinner if you need me. Will you be staying for dinner?" she asks, looking at her sons, but avoiding my gaze.

"That depends on the outcome of this conversation," Banks mutters.

"Very well," his mother sighs before leaving the room, closing the door firmly behind her.

"Why don't you all take a seat," George offers, waving his

hand to the seating area in the corner of the oversized office. "This is kind of a long story."

Never letting go of my hand, Banks tugs me to one of the chairs. Sullivan and Oliver are right beside us. We all take seats in the leather chairs. George joins us, sitting down right across from me.

"First, I have to ask, not that it matters because you know now, but how did you find out about Phoebe?" George starts the conversation.

"I found letters and some pictures in my dad's desk. Pictures with you, my dad, and Phoebe in them."

"Yes, we used to be friends growing up… all three of us. Best friends, actually."

"How is that even possible?" Sullivan asks. "How were you friends, and why is this the first time we've ever heard of it?"

"Some things are just better left in the past, son. We were just kids when we were friends. That all changed when we grew up, and friendship turned into more between Phoebe and me."

"So, you and Phoebe were together?"

He smiles, his eyes twinkling, "Yes, I was in love with her. I was her first boyfriend… or so I thought. See, your father was in love with her as well and Phoebe… well, she was in love with both of us, and that led us to the biggest mistake of our lives…" George trails off, looking out the window, his eyes turn glassy and unfocused as he speaks.

"What happened?" I ask when I can't take the silence anymore.

"We told her she had to choose one of us. We fought over her, both of us terribly jealous of the other one. We were so selfish in our fight for her that neither one of us realized how unhappy she was and how much us fighting hurt her."

"One of the letters I found said that she was pregnant…" I hold my breath, waiting for the truth to come pouring out.

"Yes, Phoebe got pregnant. She was with both of us at the time, so there was a question of who the father was for a while, but it turned out it was Lionel."

"Am I…" My voice cracks at the end. I don't know if I can ask the question out loud. It's still too surreal.

"Yes, Harlow. You are Phoebe's daughter. Your dad met his new wife when you were just a baby. I always wondered if he told you about your mother. I guess he didn't."

To my surprise, I am not as shocked as I thought I would be. I guess part of me was expecting it already. Or maybe the revelation that my life had been a lie doesn't bother me as much because in some ways my life was already a lie, it was messed up long before I lost my memory.

"You okay," Banks asks, his voice concerned and gentle as if he has this need to soothe me.

"I am, surprisingly… I'm not that shocked. I don't know, I can't explain it. I guess deep down, I already knew."

"Your father and I have had a lot of differences over the years, as you are well aware, but I can tell you that he did love your mother, your real mother… and so did I. I was devastated when she died."

"How did she die?"

George sighs deeply and leans forward. With his elbows on his knees, he lets his face fall into his hands. Clearly, he's still torn up over it. Even after all this time, he looks like reliving the memories is extraordinary hard on him.

"At the end, it was our rivalry that killed her," he admits, and the pain in his voice is almost too much for me. "She loved us both, and even though she had a child with Lionel, she would come to see me. He tried to forbid it, of course, but she was a bit untamable. That was one of the things I loved about her...like a wild horse, she would gallop wherever she pleased..." he trails off seemingly lost in his memory.

"She would frequently sneak out in the middle of the night to meet me somewhere," George continues after a while. "One of those nights she had a car accident on her way home, a drunk driver swerved into her lane, hit her straight on... she died instantly."

A tear trails down my cheek as I mourn the death of a woman I didn't know and never will. The woman who gave me life. The mother I didn't even know existed. The mother I would only ever know from stories and pictures.

"Your father blamed me, of course. If I had stayed away from her, she wouldn't have been on that road. What he didn't understand is that I tried, but she wouldn't let me go. She loved me, and she wasn't going to give me up. If your father would have accepted that fact, then she wouldn't have snuck around in the middle of the night. He tried to control her, and he drove her away with that. She would have eventually come to me anyway."

"So, you blamed each other for her death," Sullivan points out.

"Yes... it was the seed that started it all, the seed that sprouted into hate and resentment over the years and led to a rivalry that has now touched the next generation, or so I thought. Obviously, you have somehow overwritten the hatred between our families." George looks at Banks and at our intertwined fingers.

"But at what cost?" Oliver blurts out. "We were fighting

for years, Sullivan almost lost everything, Harlow has been through hell and back... Christ, she almost died, and for what? Because you two couldn't share the blame? Because from where I'm standing, it was everybody's fault."

"Maybe you're right, but you can't change the past, and I accepted that a long time ago. We can only control our own paths now and steer into the future we want. Now the question is, what kind of future do you want?"

"I want a future where I remember my past. I want to know where I came from, and I want to know where I belong," I admit.

"You belong with us," Oliver says, making his dad shift in his chair uncomfortably. I wonder if he knows what kind of relationship I have with his sons? Maybe he is trying to figure it out, or maybe he already suspected it. Either way, he is not saying a word about it.

"You know what I want for the future? I want Harlow to be safe," Banks barks. "I want Shelby and whoever has been trying to hurt Harlow behind bars for good. And then I want everybody to leave us the hell alone and let us live our lives as we please."

"Wait, why do you want Shelby behind bars? Isn't she your friend?" George asks, looking between all of us with confusion.

"I remembered something... about Shelby. She was the one that hit me with the car."

George looks genuinely shocked. "Did you go to the police?"

"Yes, we called the detective on my case. They are looking for her right now. But last we checked, they hadn't found her yet." I contemplate telling him about seeing Shelby and Dad together but decide against it. There is no real reason for him to know that part. "I wanted to talk to my dad about all of this, but the guys think it's a bad idea."

George's gaze collides with Banks' when he speaks again. "I want you to stay out of this. All of you," he looks to Sullivan and then Oliver. "I know you want to help Harlow, but you really need to stay out of it and let the police handle it."

Banks sighs beside me, his fingers tightening around mine. He doesn't answer, but I already know what he would say if he did. Something along the lines of, don't tell me what to do because I'll do what I want.

Surprisingly, Oliver is the one who speaks up. "We will do anything that we can to help Harlow. There is no staying out of it, we're already involved. Harlow's life is intertwined with our own, and we won't stand by and watch her be attacked or hurt."

George shakes his head, looking thoroughly displeased with Oliver's statement. "Are you boys staying for dinner?" George asks after the silence has stretched between us. I don't miss how he only invited the guys to dinner; does he expect me to leave?

"I think it's time for us to go," Oliver announces and shoves out of his chair. His body is vibrating with an unknown emotion. The brothers follow Oliver's lead, and I stand as well, slowly, my knees knocking together gently. I'm so exhausted.

"Thanks for the chat," Sullivan says, heading for the doors. We all follow without anyone saying a real goodbye. George stays in his office, and we don't see anyone else on the way out. The guys don't look for their mother to tell her goodbye either. It's kind of sad and fucked up and wrong, and somehow, I get it.

When we get to the car, I feel guilty. Am I the reason the guys have a bad relationship with their parents? When Oliver starts the car and pulls away, I can't wait any longer. I need to know if this is all because of me. "Do you guys fight with your parents because of me?"

"We fight with our parents because they are pricks," Banks growls, "They shouldn't treat you the way they do, they shouldn't treat anyone like that."

"But if it wasn't for me, you would be okay?"

"Harlow, don't you dare think it is your fault that we barely talk to our parents. I can assure you, it's not," Oliver promises.

"He is right, it's not on you. It's their own fault," Sullivan chimes in.

I'm not completely convinced, but it's enough for me to let it go for now. Relaxing into the leather seat, I realize how tired I am again. This meeting was emotionally draining. I unbuckle my seatbelt and lie down across the back seat, resting my head in Banks' lap. He immediately starts running his fingers through my hair, giving me a little scalp massage.

"That feels nice," I murmur before I can't keep my eyes open any longer, and I quickly fall into a deep, dreamless sleep.

5

The days with the brothers blend together, and while I'm happy and content staying with them in a rental house far away from the world, I know this won't last forever. We can't hide from everyone for the rest of our lives.

As I sit in the kitchen staring into my coffee, my mind wanders to the questions that still plague me. It's been a while since I talked to my father. He hasn't tried to contact me or seek me out, at least not that I'm aware of. Maybe the guys are not telling me that he is, which I wouldn't put past them. They want to protect me, and my father is the last person they want me speaking to.

"What are you doing, beautiful?" Sullivan's husky voice tickles my ear, and goosebumps blanket my skin at the tone.

"Thinking..." I reply, "Do you think my father knew that Shelby was the one that tried to kill me?" I can't imagine him knowing and not doing anything, then again, this is the same man that tried to marry me off to someone as if I was a business contract, and not a human with feelings, and choices of her own.

"I don't know." He plucks an apple out of the fruit basket in front of me, his toned body presses against mine, and a spark of electricity zings through me into my core. "I wouldn't be surprised if he did."

Swallowing thickly, I try and push the fluttering of butterflies in my belly away. I can't be thinking about crawling all over him when there are bigger things that I need to be thinking about.

"Eventually, I want to go back to classes, but as long as Shelby is out there, I'm not safe to do so."

"You think we would let anything happen to you?" Oliver enters the room, his laptop in his hand.

"No, but I would feel better if she was locked up. I don't know why she did the things she did, but I'm terrified of something happening again, and I can't expect one of you to always be with me." I don't try and hide my anxiety from the brothers. There is nothing to hide. They know how worried I am.

"What do you want to do?" Sullivan asks, biting into his apple.

"I don't know, but I need to find her."

"You aren't doing shit," Banks growls, walking into the kitchen, the look on his face says, *fight me, I dare you.*

"Yeah, I'm going to have to agree with Mr. Alpha over here." Oliver hooks a thumb in Banks' direction. "Over my dead body will you get within ten feet of that bitch."

All I can do is roll my eyes at their protectiveness. Like I was really going to go out and search for her? A part of me wants to find her and ask her why she did the things she did, while the other part of me is afraid to know the answer. Why would my best friend of over 10 years want to kill me? Yes, she was having an affair with my father, but that can't be it.

"I don't mean I'm going to physically seek her out."

"Better not or I'll take you over my knee," Oliver says, the tone of his voice serious, and when I look over at him, even his face says he would do it. "And I'm dead serious, Harlow, if you do something to risk your life for us or put yourself in danger, I will blister your ass so bad you won't be able to sit for a week. You mean the world to us, and losing you would kill us." His confession makes my heart beat a little faster.

"I'm not going to do anything. Don't worry, please," I murmur softly.

"Stop scaring her with your overprotective tendencies," Sullivan shakes his head and cups my cheek. Leaning in, his lips gently graze mine. He smells like apples and sunshine, and I want more. Greedily, I reach out and grab on to his shirt, clinging to him. Before I get the chance to deepen the kiss, he's pulling away. *Damn him.*

I need some air, air that isn't filled with Bishop scent, because right now my body is on fire, need pulsing through my veins.

"I'm going to go sit outside," I announce.

"I'll join you," Banks offers, but I shake my head as I get up from my chair, my coffee mug in hand.

"No, I need some time to myself," I announce, cringing as Banks' handsome face falls. "It's not you, really it's not. I just..."

"We get it, don't feel like you have to explain yourself," Oliver answers before either of the other brothers can, and I nod, sliding past Sullivan, and then Banks on the way out. Walking out the French doors attached to the kitchen, I close them behind me and settle on to the porch swing. Sullivan's phone sits heavy in my pocket. Sipping the coffee from my mug, I know what I have to do, and I hope that the brothers don't get angry with me for doing it.

I don't think they're trying to keep me away from anyone or control me. They just want to make sure I'm protected, but there isn't anything my father can do to me through the phone, and I'm done sitting around here doing nothing while hiding from the world. I need to know.

Setting my cup down, I pull out the phone and stare at the screen. It feels a little bit like I'm betraying the guys, sneaking around, and taking Sullivan's phone while he wasn't looking, but just like they are not trying to hurt me, I'm not trying to hurt them.

I type my father's name into the search bar and watch as Google pulls up multiple pages, the first one being my father's company. I look through it until I find my father's office number and dial it. A high-pitched female voice answers my call on the second ring.

"Lockwood Real Estate, how may I direct your call?"

"Mhm, hi... this is Harlow Lockwood. I was wondering if you could connect me to my dad?" The line goes silent for so long that I pull the phone away from my ear, worrying that the call got disconnected. "Hello?"

"Ah, yes. Could you hold, please?" the woman on the other end asks, sounding a bit frazzled.

"Sure." I'm immediately put on hold, classical music filtering through the line. I don't have to wait long before my father picks up.

"Harlow?" His deep voice fills my ear a second later.

"Yes, it's me."

"Christ, Harlow. Where are you? Tell me, right now," he demands as if I would tell him.

"I'm fine, thanks for asking," I answer sarcastically. "I will not tell you where I am, and I definitely do not need you to pick me up. I'm just calling to ask you one thing..."

"I already told you if you want to know about Phoebe, you need to meet me."

"I already know who Phoebe was... and that I'm her daughter." Even though I've known for a few weeks now, the words are still foreign in my mouth.

"Who told you?"

"It doesn't matter. All that matters is that you've been lying to me my whole life. But that's not why I'm calling. I just want to know one thing, and then you can go back to your perfect little life. Did you know? Did you know that it was Shelby who tried to kill me?" I hold my breath, the seconds ticking by as I await his answer.

"She wouldn't..." He finally says. "Who told you it was her? Did the Bishops tell you that? I swear, I will end them for good this time." Contempt drips from his words.

"No one told me. I remembered. She drove through the intersection right as I was crossing the street. She tried to kill me."

"No... it-it must have been an accident." My father sounds a bit flabbergasted, and for a moment, I try to figure out if he is really surprised or faking it. Then, as if he gathers his thoughts, he says with a stronger voice, "I don't believe you. You either saw it wrong, or it simply was an accident."

Now it's my turn to be flabbergasted, I can't believe him. "Are you serious, right now?" My voice rises with each word, my anger simmering, threatening to boil over. "I guess I shouldn't be surprised that you would defend her, not when she's spreading her legs for you."

"What proof do you have?" My jaw aches as I grind my teeth together.

"Proof? What proof do I need? I saw it with my own eyes. She drove through the stop sign... she sped up! She hit me with her fucking car. I know she saw me, how couldn't she?"

"Are you sure?"

"Yes, I'm sure, and if you see her, let her know the police are looking for her. I can't even go back to classes because I'm worried she's going to hurt me, or worse."

Silence lingers between us, making the space heavy.

"I... I believe you, and I'm sorry. Your mother and I have been worried sick about you. Will you please just come home?"

"No, and that woman you married is not my mother. My mother was Phoebe, who you refuse to tell me anything about. But that's okay..." I can feel the smile curving at the corner of my lips, "I went to Mr. Bishop and got all the information I need."

"Harlow," the desperation in his voice makes me pause. "I... I can't do this over the phone. We need to meet in person, and I'll tell you everything. I don't know what George told you, but I'm positive that not all of it is true."

"There is nothing left to say, and I'm not sure I would believe anything you have to say now anyway." The only reason he wants to see me in person is so he can drag me back home and lock me in my room. Does he think I'm stupid?

"I know where Shelby is," he blurts out, shocking me once again. "Would you forgive me if I tell the police where she is?"

Forgive him? I have to suppress a laugh. "How about you tell the police where she is because it's the right thing to do?"

"I'll do it, but know that I'm doing this for you. Everything I've done is for you. You're my daughter, the only thing I have left of your mother, and I can't lose you."

I wish I could believe him. I wish I could love my dad like a daughter should love her father, but too much has happened, and I don't think we can ever repair our broken relationship.

There are too many lies, too many secrets. I can't trust that he'll protect me, that he'll take care of me. The thought brings tears to my eyes. My emotions are all over the place, and talking to him isn't helping things.

"Goodbye, Dad," I say before hanging up the phone.

6

A few days have passed since the phone call with my father... a phone call that the guys still don't know about. I feel bad about hiding it, but I don't want to disappoint them or hurt their feelings either. I know they just want to protect me, but I had to talk to him.

With all of that, I find myself getting cabin fever, the same four walls of this rental house close in on me a little more every day. Crawling out of bed, I strip out of Banks' shirt and walk into the bathroom connected to the bedroom. I've been bed hopping since we got here, each brother getting their own time with me. Last night, I fell asleep on the couch and woke up in bed with Oliver, all while wearing his brother's shirt. Strange, but normal for us.

Turning the shower on, I let the bathroom start to steam up before I step under the hot spray of water, letting it massage my neck and shoulders. A moan escapes my lips as my muscles relax under the spray.

"I like that sound very much, but I'd prefer you making it while I'm in there with you," Oliver murmurs, chuckling as he does. Before I know it, he's stripping out of his clothes and joining me in the extra-large shower stall. I'm not surprised to see his cock already hard, pointing at me angrily. The veins popping out, throbbing and begging to be touched.

"That looks... painful," I say quietly.

"It is. I'm so hard it hurts. It's what you do to me, Harlow. Always. Every time I'm in your presence, my cock is hard."

"Maybe I can do something about it?" I try my most seductive voice, and judging by the growl coming from Oliver's chest, I'm doing pretty good.

"Fuck yeah," he groans as I wrap my fingers around his length. Giving him a hard squeeze, I revel in the way his eyes squeeze shut, and his hands curl into fists.

"I never thought it would be possible for me to want all three of you, but I do. Each of you do something to me that I can't explain."

Oliver's eyes open then, the brown in them almost black, leaving only a small ring of brown behind, "You make us whole." He hisses out, his muscular chest rising and falling as he inhales. There is nothing like the power I hold over these three men. The way they fall to their knees for me. Stroking him faster, I swirl my thumb over the head of his cock and down his slit. Pre-cum beads the tip, and I smear in over his length, my eyes mesmerized with the motion.

"I need to fuck you, Harlow," Oliver's voice is raw with emotions and reaches down inside of me, sinking its claws deep into my core.

"I want you so bad..." I murmur, as I release his cock, and take a step back. His eyes smolder as he stalks toward me, lifting me in one fluid motion. In seconds, I'm in his arms, my back pressed against the tile wall of the shower, my legs wrapped around his middle. His swollen cock bumps against my clit and I suck a labored breath in through my teeth. Oliver stares down at me, watching me, knowing that he holds power over my body and my heart.

"Every night...." His cock brushes against my soaked entrance, and I sink my nails into his shoulder, urging him on. "I think about stealing you from my brothers' beds to have my way with you."

Feeling as if I might die if he doesn't start fucking me, I grin and say, "You should."

That must set him off because he pulls back and slams into me, making the air in my lungs still, and my entire body shake with tremors of pleasure.

"Fuck, there is nothing like sinking into you. So tight, so warm, so fucking perfect," he pants, pistoning his hips, sinking deeper inside of me. His fingers dig into my flesh hard enough to leave bruises, and I want him to. I want him to mark me. Everything around me fades away as Oliver fucks me into oblivion. My nails rake down his chest, and he hisses at the pain.

Then he starts to swivel his hips between thrusts, the head of his dick brushing against what I now know is my g-spot.

"Ahhh, Oliver..." I mewl. Strands of wet hair stick to my face, but I couldn't care less how I look in this moment. All I can do is hold on for dear life as Oliver takes from me, fucking me to the brink of insanity. The orgasm I've been chasing for the last couple of minutes stirs deep in my core and slithers up my spine.

"I'm going to come..." I whimper, staring into Oliver's eyes. He's looking at me with a determination I've never seen, a wicked grin on his handsome face.

"Fuck yeah, you are, all over my cock…" His dirty words only add to the pleasure, and within seconds I'm going off, launching into space like a rocket. My pussy clenches around his length, and just from the grunts and pants that he's making, I know he's close, and strangely, I want his come like I've never wanted it before. I want it inside of me, marking me, claiming me.

"Fill me with your come, Oliver, fill me…" I plead through the sound of blood swooshing in my ears. With a steel grip and a growl, I'm pretty sure his brothers can hear, he comes, his thighs shaking, his head tipped back, exposing his throat. Acting on impulse, I nip at that unmarred skin and smile when I feel his cock jump inside of me.

Sucking the pain of my bite away, I wait for him to come floating back down to me. Seconds later, he's staring down at me and gently placing me back down on my feet, and with the loss of his cock inside of me, I feel like I've lost a piece of my soul.

"I love you, Harlow, and I'd love you even if you didn't fuck me like you love me back. You're it for me." He peppers kisses against my face, and I start to giggle.

"You're welcome, and the feeling is mutual, you definitely know how to make a girl feel good."

Oliver grins. "All for you, baby, all for you." He gives me one more kiss, a kiss that makes me want to climb him like a tree, and not shower at all. But then we wouldn't get anything done, and as much as I love being here with them, I really want to get back to living a normal life. So instead of begging him to take me again, I focus on washing my body and hair, and less on the pulsing between my legs.

Once we've finished showering and are dressed, we make our way out to the living room. Sullivan and Banks are already lounging on the couch, both with shit-eating grins on their faces.

They heard us, or at least Oliver.

"Have a nice shower?" Sullivan asks, chuckling.

"Yeah, did you get all clean?" Banks chimes in, "It sounded like you did."

"Yes, don't worry. I was thorough... made sure I got *every* spot clean." At Oliver's words, my face turns about five shades redder.

"Don't be embarrassed," Sullivan tells me, rubbing my back when I take the seat next to him.

"Can't help it," I say, even more embarrassed. While I've become more outspoken sexually, it's still a lot for me. After all the bullying and hate I've gotten about being with all three of them, it's hard for me to handle any type of teasing without feeling like caving in on myself.

Oliver opens his mouth, and it looks as if he is about to say something when his phone starts ringing. He takes it out of his pocket and looks at the screen with his eyebrows drawn together. "It's the detective."

Before anyone can say anything, he answers the phone, placing it on speaker for all of us to hear. "Hello..."

"Good morning, Mr. Bishop. How are you doing today?"

"Very good," Oliver answers, grinning at me while he does.

"Good, good... Is Miss. Lockwood still with you?"

"Yes, I'm here," I say before anyone else can answer.

"Great. Hello, Harlow. I hope you are doing well. I know you've been through a lot, so I wanted to call you right away to let you know that we arrested Shelby a few hours ago."

"Finally," Banks mutters under his breath.

I know I should say something. I know I should probably

be happy and relieved that I'm safe now, but for some reason, I feel neither. All I feel is the need for answers.

"Did she say why she did it? Why she wants me dead?" Not knowing has been eating me up. I thought she was my best friend before all of this, so why did she want me dead?

"No, I'm sorry. She didn't give us a real reason as to why, but she did confess to wanting to hurt you."

"You put her in jail, right?" Oliver asks impatiently. "And she won't be getting out any time soon?"

"Actually..." The detective pauses, and I feel the air in my lungs still, "She's not in jail, we had to bring her into a closed psychiatric ward after what happened."

"What? Why? What happened?" I mean, I know she had some mental issues given what she did to me, but still. A psychiatric ward seems to be a little too much.

"Harlow, do you know that it was your father who called her location in?"

Almost absentmindedly I nod, before realizing he can't see me. "Yes," I say, after a moment. "I talked to him about Shelby and..." I trail off, not wanting to say the words out loud. *Shelby and my father.* I'm still so disgusted by the thought, and now I'm even more embarrassed... embarrassed about what kind of man my father is.

"When we arrested her, and she realized that your father was the one who had called us, she had a complete mental breakdown. She was yelling and screaming, saying that she's in love with him and that she needs to kill you to have him for herself. Then she tried to hurt herself, we had no choice but to send her in to have her mental state evaluated."

"So, she'll be there for a while or what?" Banks interjects.

"They're going to do a full evaluation on her, and then make a decision, but as of right now, that's where she will be staying. If I have any further updates, I'll be sure to give you a call and let you know."

"Thank you, detective," I can't explain the pressure that's been lifted from my chest at knowing that she's somewhere far away, somewhere that she won't be able to escape from, and that my father was the one who helped put her there.

A small piece of my heart beats for the man that gave me life because, in the end, he did choose me over her, but it took all of these bad things happening to me for him to do it.

"No problem, have a good day." The line goes dead, leaving me with nothing more than my thoughts and the three men that own my heart. When I look up, I find all three of them staring at me. Each carrying their own confused expression.

"I was going to tell you," I start, a pang of guilt hitting me.

"If you wanted to call your father, all you had to do was ask. You didn't have to sneak around behind our backs." Oliver says, and the tone of his voice makes me shiver. I know without even looking at him that he's disappointed in me. Hell, I'm disappointed in me too.

"What Oliver means to say is that we want to protect you, and we can't protect you when you're doing stuff behind our backs. We're supposed to be a team," Sullivan's voice is soft and nurturing, and for some stupid reason, I want to cry. I don't understand why, but I do. When I look up from my hands again, there are tears in my eyes, and no matter how much I try and blink them away, they continue to fall.

"Fuck," Oliver mutters under his breath and comes to stand in front of me. He wraps his arms around me, and I breathe him in. My body lights up at his touch. This is what he does to me, what they all do to me.

"I'm... I'm sorry. I wasn't hiding it. I just wanted to know if he knew that Shelby was the one to hurt me. I know I should've come to you guys, but..."

"Shhh, no. I'm sorry. I didn't mean to yell at you." Oliver soothes, his hand moving up and down my back. It feels good, too good, and I let my eyes drift closed for a second.

"I don't want to disappoint you guys," I sob into his shirt.

"Shhh, baby, you're not a disappointment. You're as far from a disappointment as it gets." Banks' strong voice pierces my ears, and I feel him along my back, his hard body brushing against mine. He brushes the hair from my neck away and presses hot kisses to my shoulder and neck, sucking on the tender flesh along my collarbone. Instantly, I melt into a pile of mush, the tears stopping all at once.

"Can't cry when my lips are on you?" He teases, and I can feel my insides turning to molten lava. That connection I have to each of them burning hotter and hotter.

"No," I whisper hoarsely. I'm only vaguely aware of Oliver releasing me, and turning me to face Banks.

"I'm sorry my brothers are assholes. I'll make it up to you." Banks' pink tongue flicks out over his bottom lip, his blue eyes blazing with unbridled need beneath the amusing glint. I want to give in to him. I want to let all three of them have a chance at me all over again... but...

Out of nowhere, a wave of dizziness hits me, and I'm overcome with nausea. Bile rises up my throat, and I know what's going to happen next. Without even thinking, I shove against Banks and make it to the kitchen sink just in time to vomit up all my breakfast. My stomach twists and I continue to puke until there is nothing but green bile coming up.

"We need to get you to a doctor," one of them says, but I can't tell who it is. All I can do is focus on the stupid need to vomit. Banks takes my hair into his hands and holds it away from my face. My fingers grip on to the counter as everything pours out of me. By the time I'm done, my eyes are watering, and my throat is burning.

I know they're right; the vomiting and exhaustion aren't normal, and I should get checked out, but a part of me doesn't want to know what's wrong. A part of me hopes whatever is happening goes away. Maybe it's just stress? I mean, what else could it be?

"I think it's just stress, this is all too much…" I groan, taking the paper towel that Oliver offers me. Wiping at my mouth and eyes, I do my best to make sure that there isn't any puke on my chin or lips.

"Even if it is stress, you've been getting sick a lot lately, and it wouldn't be a bad idea to get checked out."

"What if it turns out to be something more?" I ask, fear ringing my voice. "The doctors told me that I could possibly run into more problems from the accident down the road. Maybe that's what he was talking about."

"Then we deal with it." Sullivan answers, his voice soft and warm, and all I want to do is go to him and let him wrap his arms around me.

Knowing there isn't any point in trying to fight it, I agree. "Okay, I'll make an appointment."

"Thank you, that's all we want. You are the most important thing to us, and if you're sick, then we need to find a way to fix it."

"Sometimes, things can't be fixed." I drop my gaze down to my hands. Shelby has been caught, life is good, and yet somehow it all seems temporary like at any minute the rug is going to be ripped out from underneath our feet.

Banks cups me by the cheek, and I nuzzle into his touch. "When it comes to you, everything can be fixed.

Let's get you a shower, something small to eat, and some rest."

"Sullivan and I will get everything figured out so we can go back to classes," Oliver announces.

That makes me perk up. Excitement bubbles through me. This is just what I needed to hear.

"Yes, we're finally leaving and going back to classes. Now that Shelby has been caught, we have nothing to worry about."

"We can finally all be together, and attend classes like we were meant to. Everything will go back to normal now. We'll get to be normal, or as normal as we can be as college students."

I smile because deep down, I am happy, but I can't shake the inky dread that something bad will happen. It always does. It always finds a way to ruin the good in my life.

7

"I thought you would be excited to be back in classes?" Caroline says from her seat beside me. She must see the permanent scowl that seems to have taken up residence on my face this week.

Things have pretty much gone back to normal, even Tiffany and her cronies are treating me the same as they always have, no matter how much I try to ignore their jibes, I just can't seem to. Merely thinking her name makes my brain scream.

"Earth to Harlow, you're looking at Tiffany like you want to rip out her throat, are you okay?" Caroline's soft voice fills my ears, and I look away from Tiffany before I do just that. She's bitchier than I remember her being, and it's taking everything in me to bite my tongue when she or her barbie brigade walks past me and calls me a slut beneath their breaths. It's petty and childish, and I just want them to go away.

"I'm fine, just a little... aggravated," I hiss, trying not to look in Tiffany's direction.

"Could've fooled me. I thought you were plotting Tiffany's murder there for a second."

"That's because I was." I peek up at Tiffany again. She tosses her hair over her shoulder and laughs loudly at something one of her friends says. *Bitches.* Mean stuck-up bitches. That's all they are. "I don't understand why they have to be such assholes. It's not like what I do with my life has any effect on them." I'm merely venting now, and even though I should stop and save it for when I get back to the house, it feels good to let it out right now.

At least I'll be less likely to reach out and bash Tiffany's head against the wall this way.

"She'll forever feel like you stole Oliver from her." Caroline's response makes me grit my teeth. "Before you bagged my cousins, she had her sights set on him, and from the look of it, she still does. I bet she hates you for having their hearts when she can't even get their attention. Never could. Even when they were pretending to like her, all they would talk about was you."

"Well, maybe if she wasn't being a raging bitch all the time, she could get a guy to like her for more than her mouth or the thing between her legs."

"Amen to that," Caroline mumbles. "Maybe we should tell her that..."

Grinning, I shake my head. The last thing I need is more encouragement. I spend the rest of the class trying to ignore Tiffany and concentrate on the outline for my English literature paper instead. When the professor announces we're free to go, I'm so relieved I practically sag in my seat. Who knew ignoring someone could be so draining? Then again, I guess the ignoring part wasn't my problem. It's more holding back my anger, so I don't end up getting booted from the school.

Gathering my stuff quickly, I start to get excited when I realize that I'll be seeing the guys in a few minutes. Like every day, we all meet for lunch, something that's slowly becoming my favorite part of the day.

"In a hurry to get to your *boyfriend*?" One of Tiffany's friends snarls, her voice condescending.

"Please, Claire, don't be ridiculous and call them her *boyfriends*," Tiffany decides to add her input. "She is nothing more than their little plaything. Don't you remember how they used to talk about her? How we used to make fun of her with the guys? They don't want her, at least, not like they would want you or me." I can't help myself. I look the bitch right in the eyes and just stare, wishing I could show her just how much they don't want her.

"Why don't you guys get lost," Caroline snaps. "You're just jealous because she has what you want."

"Ha, jealous? Of *her*?" Tiffany's nose wrinkles and I clench my free hand into a tight fist. *Don't slug her.* My muscles burn, as anger pulses through me. Concentrating on not wiping the smug smile off her face... with my fist.

When they move to leave, Tiffany digs her shoulder into my arm in a feeble attempt to knock me over, but my body is too rigid, and the only thing she accomplishes is making my backpack slide off my shoulder.

"Oops," she snickers and walks off as the bag slides down my arm and on to the floor.

God, I hate her.

"Congrats on having as much self-restraint as you do. I thought you were about to fight her for sure," Caroline tells me when they leave, and we are the only two people left in the classroom.

"Yeah, I'm surprised myself," I say with a shrug. "Maybe I

just didn't want to be late for lunch. I'm starving. My stomach's been growling for the last hour."

"Girl, you've been all about the food lately. That wouldn't have anything to do with you meeting the guys for each meal, would it?" Caroline giggles.

"Maybe," I grin.

We speed walk across campus to get to the sandwich shop where we are meeting the guys. As it turns out, a walk is exactly what I need. The fresh air helps me clear my head and cools my simmering anger toward that witch. When we arrive at the shop, all three of the Bishops are standing out front, waiting for us. Banks spots us first and gives me a panty-melting smile, and my mind goes blank for a moment, forgetting all about Tiffany and her group of barbies.

"Hey, you two," Oliver greets us when we are only a few feet away.

I have this animalistic urge to give each of them a kiss, but we haven't been that comfortable with public affection while we are out in the open like this, and it's not because we don't want to be seen with each other or because we're hiding that we are together.

It's more because we don't want to draw any type of attention to us, and having three boyfriends will definitely do that.

Walking into the restaurant together, Oliver spots a table in the back that will fit all of us.

"How was your class?" Sullivan asks as I take a seat and read over the menu.

Before I can answer, Caroline opens her big fat mouth, "Tiffany was being a major bitch last class, but other than that, today has been fine." I give her a side-eye.

Why can't she keep her mouth shut? This is just going to worry the guys further.

"What do you mean she was being a bitch? Is she bothering you again?" Sullivan asks concern etched into his handsome features. Part of me wants to sweep it under the rug and tell them it's nothing, but if I don't tell them and they find out later, I'll feel bad for having not been honest.

"Well, it seems as if she is under the impression, I stole Oliver from her, so she's trying, like always, to pick a fight. That's all. There's no reason to worry. Can we eat now? I'm going to eat my left arm off if I don't get something in my belly soon."

"I'm sorry, Harlow… This is all our fault," Oliver huffs, looking away from me as if he is too ashamed to look at me. My eyes catch on his shiny brown hair as he runs a hand through the thick strands. When he looks back at me, I can see the regret pooling there. "I kind of pretended to like her."

"It's in the past, this is the present, and we are only looking ahead, and from where I'm sitting, the future is looking pretty good," I smile. "I mean, I do see a delicious Italian sub in the near future…so…" The waitress must have heard me, because just then she walks up to the table, a tablet in her hand, ready to take our orders.

For the rest of our lunch together, we don't talk about Tiffany or anyone else we don't like. Everything seems to feel better when I'm with the guys. Being with them reminds me that no one here is worth risking my happiness for.

Only after I've finished every bite of my sub, do I realize that Sullivan seems oddly withdrawn, barely looking at me and not even finishing his sandwich. I'm about to ask him what's going on, when he pushes his plate away and gets up from the table, his chair scraping against the floor. My eyebrows draw together in confusion.

Where is he going?

"I'm gonna head out. I want to get to my next class a little early. I'll see you later," he doesn't really speak to anyone in particular and starts walking away before any of us can respond. It feels like someone has stabbed a tiny knife into the corner of my heart. It doesn't really hurt, but it leaves a noticeable ache behind.

That's what Sullivan has just done to me. He's left an ache behind, and I know without even asking that something is going on with him.

"What's wrong with him?" Oliver asks out loud what I was wondering silently.

Banks shrugs, clearly not worried about his brother's behavior. "His grades are probably slipping. His mind has been occupied as of late," he grins at me, and I can tell he's trying to lighten the mood. "You know how worried he gets about his perfect GPA."

"Yeah, but that doesn't mean he has to be rude," Oliver growls, shoving a spoon full of soup past his lips.

"I just hope he's okay. I'll talk to him later tonight," I announce before taking a sip of my soda.

"We better get going too," Banks leans over and whispers into the shell of my ear. His hot breath fans against my skin and goosebumps erupt across my skin. The next class we have together, and the thought leaves me feeling all warm inside. I'll be able to hold his hand for the next hour, and if that's not a good way to make it through calculus, then I don't know what is.

~

Even with Banks by my side, calculus is unbearable. Numbers are just not my thing, and while I luckily have Banks here to give me a little extra help, it's not going to help me pass the tests that I'll have to take on my own. I need to focus, to digest the words that are being spoken.

If Banks can sense my confusion and disappointment in myself, he doesn't let on. Class seems to go on forever, and come the end when I'm gathering my things, the only thing I want to do is go back to the house with the guys and sleep.

With everything in my backpack, I step into the aisle and head for the door. I've made it a total of five feet when Professor Clarkson calls my name.

Gritting my teeth, I walk to the front of the room where his desk is. As soon as I reach his desk, my stomach starts to churn. The smell of his cologne is overpowering. It's like I'm stepping into a cloud of some cheap masculine fragrance. The odor is so overwhelming that I don't even want to open my mouth and talk.

"Miss. Lockwood," Mr. Clarkson greets, "I just wanted to make sure you are doing okay with the work now. Your homework from last week was inconclusive, and you seemed to be having a difficult time in class today as well."

Great. Of course, he needs to point out how horrible I am at this.

"Yeah, I'm fine," I say, concentrating on not throwing up all over his brown suit.

He looks at me like he doesn't believe me, heck, I don't even believe me.

"Are you sure? I can recommend you to some study groups or assign you a student tutor. If you start to fall behind, catching up will be difficult, and I don't offer extra credit. I would hate for you—"

"I'll help her with her homework," Banks cuts in his blue eyes blazing. "She'll be fine."

Mr. Clarkson's eyes narrow, and it seems like he wants to say something else, but instead, presses his lips into a firm line. He stares at me for a long second before speaking again.

"Very well, then. I expect your grades to be up in the coming weeks. I'll see you next week," he says while closing his laptop.

I take that as my cue to go, and hastily leave the room holding my breath along the way. Only after I've taken a few steps into the hallway do I release the burning air in my lungs and suck in an even larger breath of oxygen.

"Hey, wait up. Are you okay?" Banks calls after me.

"I'm fine," I gasp, my lungs still burning as I lean against the nearest wall, my body swaying like a building during an earthquake. "I just couldn't stand the smell of his cologne. It was so strong, he smelled like he poured the whole bottle on himself."

"Are you sure that's it?" Banks eyes me wearily, "Because you look like if the wall wasn't holding you up that you'd be on the ground."

Letting my eyes fall closed, I focus only on my breathing for a moment. Once my chest has stopped rising and falling like I've run a mile, and my stomach isn't churning anymore, I open my eyes again. When I do, I find Banks has boxed me in with his body, his muscled arms frame my face, and suddenly my pulse starts to race for an entirely different reason. My cheeks heat at the indecent thoughts filling my mind.

Him taking me against the wall.

Me calling his name out as he brings me to orgasm over and over again....

"Is this too much for you?" Banks' husky voice fills my ears and interrupts my thoughts. He's staring at me with a hunger that only I can quench, and I want him, even now, right here in the middle of the hallway. Then it hits me, he asked me a question...

"God, no... this is... I feel better already," I whisper, just before his lips descend on mine, making any discomfort I felt moments ago vanish into thin air. He kisses me with so much love like I am the earth, and he is the sun. Like I'm his first taste of water after months of drought.

When he pulls away, I whimper and grip on to his shirt, wanting to keep him close.

"That's not what I mean, baby. I mean, me, my brothers, is all of this too much for you? All this shit with Tiffany, with our parents and yours. No one, including me, has stopped to ask how you're handling all of this. If you're okay?" He whispers the last part, his hot breath fanning against my lips as he pushes his forehead against mine.

This close I'm simply breathing him in, soaking him up like a sponge.

"Of course, I'm okay. I've wanted this, wanted each of you for so long, and I don't want to give you guys up. You're all I have left. You're the only people who care about me, who don't try and control me."

Banks' tongue dips out of his mouth and on to his full bottom lip, and all over again, my thoughts shift.

"If this ever becomes too much for you, I want you to tell me. Please, Harlow..." The desperation in his voice reaches inside me and sinks its claws into my heart.

"You'll never have to worry about that because it will never be too much for me. You and your brothers are all I want. All I'll ever need."

Banks stares at me for a long moment, his ocean blue gaze piercing my soul, fracturing it. He looks as if he doesn't believe me, and the thought of that kills me. It makes me want to die a slow and painful death. He has to know that I mean what I'm saying. My heartbeat thunders in my ears, drowning out every other sound around me.

"I love you. You believe me, don't you? That this isn't too much? That I want you and your brothers?" Air stills in my lungs while I await his response.

"I do believe you, and I love you too." His voice is soft, softer than normal, and when he presses a kiss to my forehead, it seems like everything is going to be okay. Taking my hand into his, we walk out of the building, and I feel a little better with every step I take. I don't know what's going on with me lately, but I need to figure it out. The dizziness, fatigue, and vomiting. None of it is normal, but after everything we've already been through, the last thing I want to do is add more to our already overflowing pot.

A smile pulls at my lips when the high hanging sun meets my skin. The warmth radiates through me, leaving me feeling warm all over. I can't wait to get home and relax with my guys, curled up on the couch, where no one can judge us or look down on us just for loving each other. When we are at home, it's just us, and that's the way I prefer it to be.

As we head to the car, we pass a group of people standing outside the library. Immediately, I recognize Tiffany's annoying giggle. I try to ignore her, but still can't help but glance over there. What I see has me stopping dead in my tracks.

Sullivan is standing with Tiffany and her friends. Even worse, he seems to be talking to them, saying something that made her giggle. *What the hell?*

I turn to Banks and find him staring daggers at his brother. He wraps his arm around me a little tighter than necessary, and I lean into his touch, seeking much-needed comfort. I don't know why Sullivan would do that, talk to her, befriend her, but I know that I can't stand here and watch this. I need to get away. I have to.

Luckily, Banks has the same idea. With his arm around me like a security blanket, he walks me to the parking lot, my legs move on their own, and when we get to the car, Banks helps me into the passenger seat.

"What the hell was he doing?" I ask when Banks gets into the driver's seat.

"I don't know, but he can ride home with Oliver," he grunts angrily. "Or he can stay here, for all I care."

We drive to the house in silence, every time I glance over to Banks, his face is set in stone, and he's gripping onto the steering wheel so tightly, his knuckles are completely white. I almost wish he wasn't so angry about it. I wish he would tell me that it was nothing, that Sullivan would never go behind my back. Seeing Banks so upset about this only makes this whole thing worse.

When we pull into the driveway and Banks cuts the engine, we don't get out right away. Banks take a few deep breaths like he is trying to calm himself before he opens his mouth to speak. "I'm sorry, I don't mean to be angry. I mean, I am angry, but not at you. I don't want to let my anger out on you. I don't know what the fuck Sullivan was thinking, but it really pisses me off seeing you hurt. You've been hurt enough, and it's our job to prevent you from being hurt any further." I'm still mad at Sullivan, but having Banks tell me this, has me feeling a whole lot better.

"Maybe it wasn't what it looked like. Let him come home

and explain himself before we jump to any conclusions," I suggest, and Banks nods in agreement.

"In the meantime, we do have the house all to ourselves for the next two hours." A mischievous grin spreads across his face. "What could we possibly do with all that free time?"

The mood inside the car turns swiftly. All concerns disappear and are replaced with an aching need to go inside and get undressed.

"Mhm, I'm not sure. Let's go inside and think of something. You know how I can think best?" I ask, tapping my chin.

"How is that?" Banks asks with a grin.

"Naked."

8

When Oliver and Sullivan walk through the door, Banks and I have just finished putting dinner together. The whole time we've been waiting, my emotions have been all over the place. I try not to interpret the scene I witnessed earlier wrongly; I want to talk to Sullivan before I give it any more thought.

"Hey, guys," I greet them, forcing a smile on my face.

"Hey, beautiful," Oliver says with a grin, walking up to me and kissing my cheek.

"Hey," Sullivan mutters, walking up to me next. He places a chaste kiss on my other cheek. I expect him to say something more, anything more, to explain himself, maybe even apologize. But he does none of those things. Instead, he grabs a soda from the fridge and turns his back to me. Literally and figuratively. Part of me is screaming inside, telling me that I should say something, anything.

"I'm going to head to bed," Sullivan says, out of thin air, and my hands clench into tight fists. *Of course, you are.*

"You're not gonna eat?" Oliver questions.

Sullivan shakes his head. He can't even lift his head to look at his brother as he speaks.

"Nah, I don't feel good. I'll see you all in the morning."

"No fucking way," Banks yells, causing everyone to look his way. Anger spills out of him as he lifts a closed fist, slamming it down on to the marble island. "You're going to explain to us, but more importantly, to Harlow, what the hell you were doing with Tiffany earlier?"

"What?" Oliver's eyes widen in shock. My throat tightens as I await Sullivan's answer. He still loves me, right? He still wants this? Us? All these questions hang on the edge of my tongue, but I just don't have the courage to ask them.

"I wasn't doing anything," Sullivan answers defensively. His eyes swing around the room before coming to a stop on mine. In his blue depths, I see despair and anger, "Just talking. Am I not allowed to talk to anyone anymore?"

"Jesus, what the fuck, dude?" Oliver yells, his carefree, happy mood changing with every second that ticks by.

"Just calm down, I wasn't doing anything wrong. You're blowing this whole thing up!" He growls, waving us off before walking out of the room. I listen to his footsteps as they recede into the other room and then up the stairs. My mind is blown, my heart shattered. What is going on, and how in the world am I going to fix it? Is Sullivan really befriending the one person who hates me most?

Tears well in my eyes, but I blink them away. Crying isn't going to do me any good right now. Banks curses under his breath and follows behind him, only to return minutes later.

Banks stomps into the kitchen, "He locked his door and is refusing to open it." I don't understand. How did we get here? I thought everything was good. I thought we were all happy. I must be wearing my emotions on my face because a moment later, Banks is at my side, his arm wrapping around me, "If you want me to, I can go back up there and kick the door in, but I don't think it's going to do any good."

I shake my head, "No. If he wants to talk, he'll talk. We can't make him do something he doesn't want to do, and if what he says is true, then there isn't anything more for him to say."

"Would someone tell me what the hell happened?" Oliver's gravelly voice pierces my ears, and I look over at him, nearly having forgotten he was in the room.

"It's nothing," I answer because honestly, the last thing I want to do is rip the brothers apart. They're brothers. They should be there for each other, not be at one another's necks.

"It's not nothing," Banks objects, "it's a big fucking deal, especially because it involves Tiffany."

Oliver looks between us, bewilderedly, "What did he do?"

Before I can shut him up, Banks is talking again. "We saw Sullivan, Tiffany, and her friends standing outside the library earlier. He was just standing there talking to them, and though it seems harmless, it's wrong. After everything she did to Harlow, after all the things she said, and continues to say."

I can practically feel the steam rolling off of Banks.

Oliver just stares at both of us, drinking up every word that his brother gives him.

"I'll talk to him. I'll figure out what the hell is going on." The gusto in his voice gives me hope. If anyone could talk some sense into Sullivan, it would be his oldest brother, but even if he does, it doesn't really change anything. Sullivan still made the choice to converse with Tiffany, and I can feel him pulling away from me. Putting distance between us.

Oliver dishes up the meal, and the boys dig in, but all I do is stare down at my plate.

We're all supposed to be sitting down to eat, but instead of being together, it feels like we're falling apart, and there isn't any way I can stomach a meal with the way I'm feeling right now. Not with the amount of distance and tension between us all tonight.

"I think I'm just gonna head to bed," I say, shoving the food on my plate around with a fork.

"You sure? You haven't eaten anything," Banks says, placing his hand on my arm.

"Yeah, I'm fine. I just want to go to sleep and let this day be over with." Hopefully, tomorrow will be a better one.

"Why don't you two go on to bed. I'll clean this up and join you in a few," Oliver suggests with a smile, and I'm all for that. Banks nods and gets up with me. Together we climb the stairs and enter his bedroom.

He sets me on the bed and helps me undress before undressing himself. I'm so upset I can't even fully enjoy the little striptease he's giving me. When we are both mostly naked, he climbs on the bed and pulls me down next to him. Spreading the blanket over us, he tucks me into his side, and I bury my face into his chest. He smells like soap and man. Slowly his body heat seeps into mine, and I relax deeper into the mattress.

I'm almost asleep when the door creaks open, and light from the hallway spills over into the room. I glance up, hoping it might be Sullivan after all, he's never gone to bed without saying goodnight to me first. When I see that it's Oliver instead, a slight wave of disappointment washes over me, and my heart stills in my chest.

Why is he doing this?

I try to push it away, the pain, the anger. I try to be happy that Oliver is here, as he climbs into the bed and lies down next to me. As he wraps his arm around me and cuddles me. I know I'm being ridiculous and spoiled.

Here I am with two guys, two men that love me, but still, I can't be happy about it because I'm missing a third. Sullivan is meant to be here, and without him, it feels like there is a huge piece of who I am, who we are, missing.

I just can't help it... no matter how much Oliver and Banks mean to me, I don't feel complete unless I have Sullivan too. Having him pull away from me... away from us, it hurts. It hurts more than anything else I've been through thus far.

∽

THE NEXT TWO days aren't any better, unfortunately. Sullivan seems isolated and cut off from his brothers, and I. Annoyance slowly turns to jealousy as I try and figure out why he's changed so suddenly. One minute everything was fine, and the next, he's avoiding me at every turn. He doesn't even look at me anymore, and if I try and speak to him, he pretends as if he hasn't heard me. It's like he is actively trying to distance himself from me.

All morning, I was looking forward to our afternoon class together, hoping that maybe then he would talk to me, but as I sit in the classroom waiting for him, the seat next to me remains empty. Of course, he would ditch me.

Chewing on the end of my pencil, I look around the class absentmindedly, because let's face it, I won't be able to concentrate on anything written on the whiteboard anyway.

When nothing inside the classroom holds my interest, I let my gaze wander to the windows.

For the next few minutes, I let mother nature calm my mind a little as I watch how the wind makes the leaves dance in the trees. I'm finally starting to breathe a little better, the ache in my chest easing a bit when my gaze catches on something in the distance.

For a moment, I just stare, my mood souring as I watch Tiffany walk out of the building across the street and down across the lawn. When I spot Sullivan walk up and greet her, that sour mood turns to red hot anger.

Leisurely, he strolls beside her, as if they're the best of friends. Of course, I can't hear what she is saying, but from her body language, I can tell that they are having a friendly conversation... too friendly when it comes to her. Maybe I wouldn't react this strongly if it was somebody else... anybody else. But *Tiffany*? It feels like a thousand tiny knives are stabbing at my heart right now.

He skipped class with me to meet up with her?

Jealousy burns through me, rushing to the surface, leaving a bitter taste on the tip of my tongue. Unshed tears sting my eyes as I gather up all my stuff and shove everything inside my bag. I can't do this right now. Not ever actually. The professor briefly glances up at me but doesn't say anything as I get up and start descending the steps. I can feel eyes on me as I reach the doors and escape the confines of the room.

By the time I make it down the hall, the tears have started to fall, each one leaving a stain against my cheek. My vision goes blurry, either from all the tears or something else. Before I can grasp what is happening, my head is spinning, or maybe it's the world around me. I can't really tell. It feels like I'm on a roller coaster, my body going up and down, up and down.

On autopilot, I reach into my back pocket and fish out my phone. Unlocking it, I scroll to Oliver's number. With my eyes closed, I hold the phone to my ear and wait for Oliver's voice to fill my ear. The sound of his voice instantly calms me, grounds me, reminds me that everything is going to be okay.

"Can you come and get me," I ask, breathlessly. "Building eleven."

"Is everything okay?" I can hear the concern etched into his vocal cords.

"Yeah, can you please just come get me." The floor sways beneath my feet, and I'm not sure how much longer I can hold on.

"Of course, I'll be right there." He hangs up before I can say anything else, and all I can do is hope that I'll be okay, that everything will be okay. Because if it isn't, I'm not sure what I'll do.

9

"You need to tell us, right fucking now, what you were doing with Tiffany?" Oliver speaks through his teeth, greeting Sullivan as soon as he enters the living room. Of course, my body starts to physically ache when our eyes lock. His brows pinch together with worry as he looks between his brothers and me. Oliver is next to me on the couch, Banks on the other side, both of them are holding on to me, holding me together.

"What's wrong? Are you okay?" Sullivan questions urgently, looking directly at me. He sounds almost frantic, and though I want to tell him, to reassure him that everything is okay, it's not. With everything going on, with all the added stress. It's wearing me down. Eating away at my resolve.

"Since when have you earned the right to ask her a question? She's been trying to talk to you all week, and all you do is ignore her." Banks lashes out at Sullivan next. Deep down, I don't want them to fight, even over me.

"Harlow," Sullivan takes a hesitant step toward me, and I

can't stop the tears from forming in my eyes. I blink them away, but they remain there, a reminder of how out of control my emotions have become. "Are you okay? What happened? Tell me, and I'll make it better. I'll do whatever I need to fix it."

To fix it. For some reason, my ears catch on those three words.

"Do you want her? Do you not want..." The words lodge in my throat. After everything we've been through, the mere thought of us not all ending up together. It kills me, physically kills me.

Sullivan looks as if I've slapped him, his nostrils flare and his eyes flicker with anger.

"Who? Tiffany?" All I can do is nod.

His body visibly trembles, and in nothing more than a second, he's crossed the space separating us. "No, no way in hell. I don't want her. You've got it all wrong. I don't give a fuck about her. I've been trying to get close to her, so I can find out what she's doing and who she's been talking to."

What? I don't understand.

"What are you talking about?" Banks asks the same confusion filling his face as mine.

"Last week, I went to talk to her to tell her to leave you alone. She told me that she's not the one we need to worry about; that there were other people looking for Harlow, asking questions about her..."

"And why the hell didn't you tell us any of this?" Oliver yells, his cheeks heating.

"Because I didn't know if Tiffany was even telling the truth or if she was just trying to get to us. I didn't want to worry you, Harlow." Sullivan's gaze drops to the floor, and I swear it feels like I can breathe again. At least now, I know he didn't really want her. He was only doing it to protect me.

"I guess I worried you just as much by not telling you what I was doing," he says, sounding completely defeated.

Before I know what is happening, Sullivan pushes the coffee table out of the way and is on his knees at my feet. His hands move up my legs, coming to rest on my hips, where he gives me a firm squeeze. Burying his face into my jean covered thighs, he inhales, and I do the same, moving my hand to his head, so I can thread my fingers through those long chocolate brown locks.

Suddenly my entire world realigns, and it's like all the planets in my solar system are back in order and no longer on a course for collision.

"I'm so sorry, baby, so sorry..."

"It's okay, but you could've told me. I would've understood."

Sullivan lifts his head, a dimpled grin appearing on his lips, "But would you have? If I had told you what I was going to do, you would've freaked out and told me not to, and while it was hard as hell not to look at you or tell you what I knew. I needed to be strong if I wanted answers."

Nibbling on my bottom lip, I nod my head, "You're right. I wouldn't have let you do it because we're a team, and we're supposed to do this all together. What if something happened to you? I thought..." I force air into my lungs, so I can say what I need to. "I was sure you were done with me."

Sullivan stares at me in shock like he can't believe I would think something like that. His blue orbs are bright, and brim with sadness, a sadness that I'm sure is reflecting back at him equally.

Turning to Oliver, I say, "Can I have a moment alone with him?"

Oliver nods his head, and then I turn to Banks. He looks at his brother with a mixed bag of emotions before speaking. "We'll leave you guys alone for a little bit." Banks narrows his eyes at Sullivan. "But if you make her cry again, I will personally rip one of your balls off and play golf with it."

Oliver snorts and releases me to get up off the couch. "You don't even play golf."

Banks chuckles, "Yeah, I know, but that's beside the point."

Each of them, press a kiss to my forehead before disappearing out of the room, leaving Sullivan and me completely alone.

"Why would you think I was done with you?" he asks.

I shrug, "I'm used to people who I thought loved me, turning their back on me. I didn't want to think the worst, but it's hard when I've been disappointed so many times. My own parents got tired of me, so it's hard to believe that you guys wouldn't."

"I'm so sorry, I didn't think about it that way. I would never be tired of you, and as for your parents... well, there is seriously something wrong with them, so you can't use them as an example.

"Honestly, Harlow, the last few days were horrible for me. I was so wrapped up in finding out what was going on, so I can protect you, that I thought it was better to keep my distance. But I didn't think me distancing myself from you was going to be a big deal for you."

"Why would you think that? I was miserable the last few days."

"Well, I thought, since you still had Banks and Oliver, you wouldn't be alone, and you wouldn't miss me much."

"Sullivan, that's not how this works. I need you; I need all three of you, and I love you. When you are not here, I don't feel complete, it's like a part of me is missing. Promise me you won't do this again."

"I promise you, I won't do anything like this again, and I will never be tired of you."

"Good," I say, leaning down and kissing the top of his head. "'Cause I will never be tired of you either. Now can you please tell me what Tiffany said that has you so worried about me?"

"I will, I swear, but first, I need you to do something for me," he says, lifting his head to look up at me.

"Anything," I say without thinking.

A wicked grin spreads across his face. "I was hoping you'd say that. God, I missed you so much." With his hands moving up my body, sparking a fire of pleasure, he presses his lips to mine. The kiss consumes me, and I claw at his shirt like a ravenous animal.

In seconds, he has me in his arms, flipping us around, so he is sitting on the couch, and I'm on his lap, straddling him. I need him right here, right now.

"I want to take my time with you, but I can't. I need you now." He groans into my neck, and my heartbeat spikes, my insides turning to liquid.

"Same. I need you just as badly," I mumble as we take each other's clothes off before finally coming together. Sinking down onto his cock, I revel in the way it spreads me, the girth of his cock filling me as my channel swallows every inch of him.

I'm mesmerized by the pleasure, consumed with a fiery

need. Sinking my nails into his flesh, I watch as his head tips back against the couch, his fingers grab onto my hips with bruising force, and strangely that's what I want. I want Sullivan to leave his mark on me.

The bite of pain leaves me greedy with need, and I start to rise, only to slam back down. I keep my pace slow, enjoying the way the head of his cock brushes against the tender tissue at the top of my pussy. With every slide down his length, I can hear our combined juices coming together, coating both of us.

"So, fucking beautiful, so fucking mine." Sullivan's words hold me hostage and encourage me all at once. Bouncing up and down on his length, I swivel my hips, and we both sigh at the ripples of pleasure that zing through us. Our bodies are like livewires, the energy between us teetering near explosive.

Sullivan must feel the heat, the pleasure rising, because with a feverish need, he threads his fingers into my hair and pulls, forcing my lips to his. He nibbles on my bottom lip, all while jackhammering upward, thrusting into me so hard that if it weren't for his grip on me in that moment, I would be off his lap.

My core clenches, pulses, and I know I'm nearing the edge of the cliff, slowly inching closer with each thrust.

"I'm close," I pant, bucking my hips, needing more, always more. I'm sure Banks and Oliver can hear us now, our sounds spilling over into other parts of the house, but I don't care, and I don't think they do either.

"Yes, come on my cock, squeeze me, let me feel you when you fall apart." He growls against my lips, and my eyes flutter closed, but only for a moment as he tugs at my hair, forcing me to open my eyes again.

"I want to see you when you come, see the heat in your cheeks, the color of your eyes. I want to see what I do to you..."

"Shit," I'm fumbling, swiveling my hips feveriously, searching for that spot, that one single... when I feel his thumb press against my swollen clit, it's all I need to push me over the edge. My eyes widen, and my mouth forms that perfect O you always hear about. Sullivan watches me intently like a man on a mission.

Like a kite in the sky, I soar into the air, riding the waves of pleasure, floating away without a care in the world. My orgasm causes a chain reaction, and as I start to come, so does Sullivan, his cock slamming into me ferociously, until I'm positive I'll still be feeling him tomorrow. His eyes remain on mine, though, unfocused, and I bare down, squeezing his length, ensuring that he's lodged deep inside of me.

A second later, sticky warmth coats my insides, and I shiver as I slowly come down from the high of my orgasm.

"I'm sorry," Sullivan shudders beneath me.

"Don't be. I love you, and it's in the past now." I nuzzle into his chest as he wraps his arms around me. With him and his brothers, I feel invincible like I can do anything, but without them, I feel broken. Like I'll never amount to anything. I know I shouldn't rely on them as my sole reason for happiness, but they're the one and only choice I've ever been able to make.

"It isn't fully in the past. There are still things we need to talk about, but none of that matters right now. The only thing I care about is getting you upstairs so we can do this all over again."

Pulling away just enough to look at him, I smirk, "Ready again so soon?"

That grin, it's the same one he's always given me, the one that makes my knees weak, and my heart do somersaults in my chest.

"When it comes to you, Harlow, I am willing and ready for anything... anytime."

And if those aren't the truest words I've ever heard, I don't know what is. There isn't anything the brothers won't do for me, and there isn't anything I won't do for them, and if we want to make it through this, if we want our happily ever after, we're going to have to continue down this path.

We're going to always have to be each other's support system.

10

The next morning, we all take a seat at the kitchen table. After Sullivan and I caught up on a week of missed sex, we were too exhausted to talk about the whole Tiffany thing, but we can't put this off any longer.

"Start from the beginning," Oliver orders, looking at Sullivan.

"Like I already said, it started with me going to Tiffany just to tell her to leave Harlow alone. When I did, she told me that I shouldn't be worrying about her when there were bigger things going on. Supposedly, there are these guys looking for Harlow. I asked her what the hell she was talking about, and she went on to tell me that there have been these rough-looking guys on campus asking around about Harlow."

"What kind of guys?" Banks asks.

"Well, that's what I've been trying to find out. Every time I talk to Tiffany, she only reveals a little bit. It's clear she was enjoying having me around, so she made sure she only gave me a smidge of information each time I saw her. She told me if I wanted any more information, I needed to be *nice* to her." Annoyance laces his words, and I can only imagine how hard this must have been for him. I hate Tiffany, hate her so much right now.

"I wasn't even sure if she was telling the truth or just playing games, but the more I listened to her and talked to others, her friends and a couple of guys around campus, the more I started to believe her."

"Fuck," Oliver says under his breath.

"According to Tiffany, these men were showing pictures of you and asking what classes you had, and where you were staying. I was so consumed with finding them that I even talked to campus security, but like I expected, they completely brushed me off. I'm pretty sure they think I'm some crazy, overprotective boyfriend now." Sullivan sighs, and all over again, I want to crawl into bed with him and forget about our crazy life. But I can't ignore this, no matter how much I want to. Someone is out there looking for me, and I don't know why.

"Do you think my dad sent them?"

Sullivan shakes his head, "I don't know why he would. I mean, he knows where you're staying, right?"

I nod, "Yeah, you're right... but who else would be looking for me, and why?"

"I don't know, but I think we should consider hiring some kind of security again. Just to make sure you are safe in the moments that we aren't with you." It's a shame Milton is in hiding.

Frowning, I say, "I had hoped that we were past this, but it seems like every time things start to get better, something has to happen. I just want to be happy."

"You can still be happy. We're all together in this, Harlow.

Where you go, we go. If we have to hire a little more protection, then that's what we do. Like always, your safety is the most important thing to us." Oliver speaks this time, giving me a dazzling smile that melts my heart.

"I know, but when does this stop, when do we get to be normal people. I'm not anything special, and yet I've come closer to dying more than the average person."

Banks laughs, "Well, I can tell you right now you're pretty fucking special. As for why people are out to hurt you, no one really knows why people do the things they do. Shelby is just mental, and now that she's been put away, the biggest risk is gone. Now, we just have to figure out who these guys are and what they want?"

Oliver places a hand on my shoulder and gives it a gentle squeeze. "Everything is going to be okay. Nothing is going to happen to you. Not now, not ever."

Just as I'm starting to calm down, and feel a little better about the shit storm called my life, a knock sounds against the door. The brothers exchange a look before Oliver pushes away from the table. The loss of his touch leaves me cold, and for some unknown reason, this inky dread starts to tug at me. I'm not sure why, but it feels like something bad is about to happen.

Sullivan moves closer to me, and Banks watches Oliver as he walks slowly to the front door. The knocking grows louder, harder, more insistent. Whoever is on the other side of that door is growing more impatient by the second.

"Are you guys expecting someone?" I ask Sullivan, just as Oliver makes it to the door.

"No, which is why I don't have a good feeling about this." His words have barely left his mouth when I look up and see Oliver opening the door. All hell breaks loose then. Immediately the door is forced open, knocking Oliver back against the wall.

I stand up so fast, the chair I was sitting on falls back and crashes to the floor. My head is dizzy, and fear has a tight grip around my throat, making it hard to breathe. I want to go to Oliver, but that would only put me in danger.

Two large men dressed from head to toe in black enter the house. One of them closes the door behind him, while the other one pulls out a gun and aims it at Oliver's chest.

A gun. No, no, no.

One of the intruders starts yelling something, but somehow my brain can't decipher what he's saying. My hands start to shake, and my lips wobble. Maybe I'm in shock, or maybe it's the fear I have of watching someone I love being hurt or worse.

Banks grabs me and shoves me behind him and Sullivan, building a wall in front of me. Because they are so much taller than me, I can barely look past them and over their shoulders, but that doesn't mean I'm panicking any less. In fact, my panic has reached new heights, because now that I don't have a clear view of what's happening, I don't know if Oliver is okay, or if one of these men are coming for Banks or Sullivan.

"Everybody, calm down," a gruff voice orders. "You do what we say, and no one needs to get hurt. You do the opposite, and well, I'm sure you know what's going to happen." A coldness sweeps through me, and I do my best to continue breathing, tiny little black spots form over my vision, the bubbling panic residing inside me is only getting worse.

"What the hell do you want?" Banks speaks, his tone defensive.

"Right now, I want everybody to slowly grab a chair and

sit down with your back against that wall over there." Peeking around Banks, I can see that the man is pointing to a spot in the dining room. "We're going to have a nice little chat."

I try to step around Banks and Sullivan, but they don't let me pass. They're like an immovable mountain. Instead, they push me back against the wall, keeping me shielded from the man making demands.

"Just relax and take a seat," a second voice orders, and only then does Banks pull up a chair and motion for me to sit down. Oliver comes up on the other side with two more chairs, a menacing look in his eyes. A moment later, all four of us are lined up against the wall.

The two men each grab their own chairs and sit down in front of us, with their guns in their hand, but they're not pointed at us, not right now, at least. My eyes stay trained to the weapons. I know it wouldn't take much to raise a hand and shoot one of us. *All of us.* Just the thought of it has my heart beating against my ribcage with the force of a sledgehammer.

Now that I have a better view of the men, I allow myself to take a good look at them when they're facing away. Both of them are tall and muscled like brick walls.

Something tells me they probably don't need those guns to inflict major damage on their enemy. One of them has a huge scar across his face, making him look like some kind of ancient gladiator. The other one has tattoos all over his hands, neck, and even some on the side of his face. At a glance, I can tell you that I would turn and walk the other way if these guys approached me at any time.

My breathing is ragged, and even I can tell I'm close to passing out.

"You need to calm down, or you're going to hyperventilate," one of the men barks. I can feel his dark gaze on me, and that only makes matters worse.

"What do you want?" Oliver grits out, diverting the attention away from me.

"We've been made aware that you four have been making threats against our boss, and we do not take threats of any kind lightly."

"There must be a mistake, we don't even know who your boss is, so how the hell could we possibly be making threats to him," Sullivan interjects, and I want to tell him his condescending tone isn't going to help us, but I can't even get my lips to move.

"No?" The guy with a million tattoos cocks his head to the side. "Your little girlfriend here should know. Or are you denying having a video of your father and Xander Rossi doing *business*?"

Business? The way he says it. In an instant, everything comes crashing into me. Just when I thought I couldn't get any more scared, the name Xander Rossi is mentioned. *Shit.* That is who sent these men. That is who is looking for me.

Somehow finding my voice, I say, "I- I wasn't threatening him. I just wanted my father to leave me alone."

Scar face smiles, and maybe it's meant as an actual smile, I don't know. But it's menacing like if a lion showed you its teeth right before ripping you to pieces.

"We don't really give a fuck what your motives were. Fact is, you have something you shouldn't have, and we are here to collect it."

"That's all you want? The video?" I force the breathless words out.

"Yup, that's all, sweet cheeks," tattoo guy winks, and I

hear Oliver grunt next to me, making the two men chuckle.

"You can have it," I tell him, "it's on my laptop in my room." I point up the stairs. "And there is a copy on a thumb drive on my desk too."

"There is a copy in my dresser as well, bottom drawer on the right," Oliver admits.

Scar face nods toward his friend, who gets up and heads up the stairs.

"You sure it's not anywhere else? Some place online, maybe? On one of your computers?" His gaze sweeps over Sullivan and Banks.

"No, that's all we've got," Banks snarls, and I can see from the way he's sitting with his back ramrod straight, his muscles straining, and his fists clenched tightly that he's barely dealing with these guys without losing his shit.

"Look, we won't release it," I assure him, surprised at how strong my voice sounds. "We really weren't going to use it to hurt your boss. I just wanted something against my father, that's all. I can see now that we made a mistake. We don't want any trouble, we told you where it is, and we'll even help you destroy all of the files."

The guy in front of us nods and strokes his chin as if he's thinking about something intently. A moment later, tattoo guy returns, holding three laptops in his arms.

"That's all I could find," he tells his friend.

"And the thumb drive?" Scar face pins me with a look.

"It was on my desk, and I haven't touched it since I put it there." Terror starts to take root again. It has to be on the desk, that's the last place I put it. The thought of it not being there, oh, god. I can't think about that...

He turns back to his partner, who gives him a head shake.

"Okay, let's go for a walk, blondie. You can find the drive for me, and we can get the hell out of here."

"No, you can't take her..." Banks shoves from his chair but is immediately pushed back down when scar face crosses the space and presses the barrel of his gun into his chest. A gasp catches in my throat. Time seems to stand still. My entire body starts to shake, and I already know the image before me is one I'll never be able to forget.

Leaning into Banks' face, the crazed man whispers, "I didn't ask what you want. I *said* I'm taking her with me upstairs to find the drive. As long as I find it, no one gets hurt. I'll return her back to you without a single hair out of place." He gestures to the other guy to come over by us. "You just sit tight and don't make any more stupid choices, and she'll be just fine."

Banks doesn't say anything, thankfully. I'm not sure that I would be able to protect him, to save him if he did something stupid right now.

When scar face moves the gun away and points it back down at the floor, I finally start breathing again. Sucking in a ragged breath, I push from the chair and slowly come to stand. My legs wobble, and Oliver wraps an arm around my hip to steady me. I don't dare look at him. The thought of something happening to them because of me... I would never forgive myself.

On shaky legs, I walk out of the kitchen without looking back. I don't have to turn around to know the man is walking behind me. In that moment, all I can hear is my thundering heartbeat and the sound of his heavy footsteps against the wooden floor.

Grabbing onto the railing to steady myself, I climb the stairs, but the crushing fear makes my head spin, and I have to stop once I reach the top step. A wave of dizziness overcomes me, threatening to pull me under and into the maddening darkness.

All at once, I'm swaying like a tree branch caught in a storm. I can feel the railing in my clammy grip. Blinking away the dizziness, I try and steady myself, but my legs are still wobbling, my knees knocking together. When the guy behind me places a gentle hand on my shoulder to steady me, I almost let out a scream. If I didn't think I might tumble down the stairs right this second, I would shove him away.

"Just take it slow and find me that drive. No need to get yourself all worked up, sweetheart. I'm not going to hurt you unless I absolutely have to."

"What about the guys? Are they safe? Are you going to hurt them?"

"Only if they do something stupid. Now isn't the time to be a hero. As long as they follow directions, I promise nothing bad will happen."

I swallow down my fear and give him a tiny head nod. Taking the last step up, I start down the hall and into my room. My feet are heavy as I head straight for my desk. With trembling fingers, I open the top drawer searching frantically for the drive. Pens, pencils, sticky notes, everything inside that drawer goes flying.

Every second I can't find it feels like an eternity. Fear rapidly mounts, and for a moment, I wonder if maybe it's lost.

What happens if I don't find it? No. I can't think like that. I'll find it. No matter what. When my fingers scrape against the back of the drawer, I start to think of another place I might have put it... but as I move across the back, and to the other side, my fingers graze against something metal and tiny.

Sweet baby Jesus.

Wrapping my fingers around the small device, I almost sag to the floor in relief. "Here it is. That's it," I'm basically panting as I hand it to him.

He smiles, and it leaves me feeling cold rather than warm. "There you go. See, that wasn't so hard, was it? Let's go back downstairs. You walk ahead of me," he orders and points his gun toward the door. I'm only feeling a little better as I walk out of the room, down the hall, and then the stairs. When we enter the kitchen again, I find all three brothers staring at me. One gaze more intense than the next, and I force the tiniest smile because right now, that's the only way I can let them know that I'm okay.

"Got it," scar face tells tattoo guy, a satisfying grin appearing on his lips.

"Great. Well, thanks for having us over at such a late hour," the man snickers. "I hope it goes without saying that we were never here, the video never existed, and you forget the name Xander Rossi for good. I don't have to tell you what happens if you don't, right?"

"We'll be happy to forget this whole thing," I say quickly, wanting this moment to end.

"Perfect. You mind seeing us out, lover boy?" he asks, looking to Oliver. The way he's looking at him gives me the creeps and makes me feel like something bad is going to happen. Everything inside me tells me not to let Oliver go with him, but as Oliver gets up from his chair, I find that I'm stuck in place, my feet sinking into the wooden floor like it's quicksand.

With Oliver leading the way, I watch as the three men walk to the door, the dreadful feeling that something bad is about to happen only expands with each step they take.

Just before Oliver reaches the door, scar face steps in his way, and without saying a single word, he pulls his fist back and punches Oliver in his stomach, the force of the blow causes him to stumble backward.

"What the fuck?" He wheezes out, doubling over, pain etching deep into his features. He wraps an arm around his stomach just as the second guy delivers another hit, this one onto the back of his head. Oliver slumps forward, landing on the floor in a heap.

My heart sinks into my stomach. I have to do something. Looking to Banks and Sullivan for some type of guidance they both wince, and give me a head shake. I can see they want to do something, but the risk of me getting hurt outweighs what Oliver is going through to them. I don't care, though, not with Oliver on the floor.

"Stop!" I scream, and jump up from the chair, my body floods with adrenaline, letting me move at speeds I didn't know were possible. I'm across the room in seconds, but the guys are right behind me, grabbing me by the arms, and hauling me backward before I can tend to Oliver.

Scar face swings around then, pointing his gun at us. He shakes his head as if I've somehow disappointed him by not staying in my seat.

"Stop, you promised you wouldn't hurt them!" I yell, my vision blurring from the onslaught of tears. I struggle against Banks and Sullivan, but there's no point. Their hands are like heavy iron shackles around my limbs.

"I promised nothing bad was going to happen. This isn't that bad... not considering what we could have done to you for threatening the Rossi family."

More tears slip down my cheeks, my chest rising and

falling rapidly as I watch them land another kick to Oliver's stomach.

"Okay, okay, you made your point. Please, just... just leave," I barely get the words out as I speak between sobs. "I swear, it will never happen again."

Scar face lifts his hand, and his partner stops mid-kick. "Next time, it won't be a little ass-kicking. Next time you'll pay in blood."

"We understand," I pant. All I want them to do is leave so I can take care of Oliver. Staring at his unconscious body, all I can think is how this is my fault, if I hadn't threatened my father then maybe none of this would have happened. This is my fault, all mine.

"Excellent," scar face smiles, and gestures for the other guy to come over by him. "It was a pleasure doing business with you. Have a good rest of your night."

Together the two men leave as if they were never here. As soon as the door closes behind them, Sullivan and Banks release me.

"I'll lock the door," Sullivan tells Banks, "make sure he's okay."

The guys bustle around me, but I'm too consumed with a need to get to Oliver that I don't even pay attention to what they're doing. Scurrying across the floor, I drop down to my knees near Oliver's head. A whimpered sob escapes my lips when I see his face. He looks as if he's sleeping, no pain on his features, but I know once he wakes up, he is going to be in a world of hurt. I just hope he is going to be okay... he has to be.

Holding his head in my lap, I run my hand over his forehead before spearing my fingers through his hair. I find a bump right away, and do my best not to press against it.

"He's got a pretty good bump on his head," I tell Banks, who is kneeling on the floor beside me. He's got Oliver's shirt pushed up, and I try my best not to flinch when I see that his ribs are already swelling, taking on a deep red, bluish color.

"He's got some bruising, but he'll be okay. He'll be in a lot of pain, but he'll live," Sullivan tells both Banks and me, and even though, I know he'll be okay, it doesn't make the fact that none of this would've happened had it not been for me, any easier to handle.

"This is my fault, all mine. I'm sorry...I'm so sorry, Oliver." I start to sob uncontrollably, my heart crumbling in my chest.

"Stop, Harlow. Don't blame yourself. None of this is your fault. Not every bad thing that happens is your fault." Banks tries his best to soothe me, his voice soft and kind, but I don't want to hear him tell me it's not my fault, not when I know deep down it is.

"This could've been much worse, so we're lucky that it ended like this, and not with you hurt, or one of us dead. People get their houses broken into all the time." Like always, the guys pretend that these bad things would've happened to them even if I wasn't part of their lives. This wasn't a random break-in. These people were here because of me. I'm a poison, destroying and infecting everything in my wake.

Holding Oliver's head in my trembling hands, I pray he wakes soon, and that I can find a way to make the Bishops' lives safe again.

Every time I need saving, they're there for me, rescuing me like white knights, but I don't want to be a princess that needs to be saved anymore.

I want to save myself and them.

11

"Would you stop, you're worse than a mother hen." Oliver slaps at my hands as I inspect his ribs for the fiftieth time today. The guilt of what happened a few days ago is still fresh. Like a newly stitched wound, it stings and burns.

"I'm sorry," I pout, "I just feel terrible about what happened, and you wince every time you walk. It makes me…"

"Stop," Oliver orders his voice strong, powerful, and way too loud for the library. "You've been beating yourself up for days over this, and it's not your fault." Leaning into my side, he twirls a strand of my hair around his finger. "I'm glad it was me. I would much rather feel this than ever see you bruised and in pain. If it were you that was hurt, you know damn well my brothers, and I would most likely be dead by now, trying to kill those fuckers."

I shiver involuntarily, the gruffness of his voice, the truth in his words. They light a flame of pleasure in my core. I still want to be the one to rescue myself, but there isn't any harm in letting a man cherish my body, my heart. Or letting three do so, all at once.

"I know, you've said that a few times now, but I still feel bad."

"Well, don't... in fact..." He presses a kiss to the sensitive spot right below my ear, and I already know what he's thinking. Mostly because I'm thinking it too. Tenderly he sucks on the flesh, and I find my fingers circling around the pencil a little tighter.

"I can't focus with you doing that..." My voice is breathless, my thoughts swirling, heading to a place that involves both of us naked, sweating, and not doing homework.

"That's the point, baby," he whispers into the shell of my ear, before scraping his teeth across the flesh that he just sucked on. The sensation is like fire and ice. Pain and pleasure.

My nipples harden against the fabric of my bra, and I drop my pencil. Oliver lets out a low chuckle, and together we shove everything into our backpacks. Before I can start walking toward the exit, he takes my hand in his and tugs me toward him.

Giving him a confused look, I let him guide me wherever it is he wants to take me. A short walk later, we're in what looks to be an upper part of the library. Old books surround us, and dust clings to the air like it's a second skin. Oliver pulls me over to a door that has a little sign on it that says DO NOT ENTER.

"What are we doing?" I whisper, afraid that we'll get caught being somewhere that we clearly shouldn't be.

"Fucking," Oliver grins at me over his shoulder, "that is if you want to." The way his teeth sink into his bottom lip, and the deepness of his voice as he speaks, it all acts as a firework to my already throbbing center.

Closing the door behind us, I don't wait to ask him any more questions. I want him, and I want him now. Like a hungry kitten, I pounce, gently shoving him against a nearby bookcase. He grins down at me, two beautiful dimples appearing on his face.

"You're so fucking beautiful and perfect, Harlow. I know you think that everything bad that happens is your fault, but you don't see the joy that you bring. You don't see how happy you make us; how much better our lives are because of you."

I gasp, because his words touch me, not in a sexual way, but in a way that makes the gnawing guilt a little more bearable.

"I don't deserve you," I whisper, pushing up on to my tiptoes. Slanting my lips against his, I kiss him with a hunger that rivals all others. And he gives it right back to me, biting at my bottom lip, and squeezing my hips in a way that makes me groan deeply into his mouth.

Our tongues collide, and in this moment, he's thunder, and I'm lightning. The perfect elements for a storm. Brushing my chest against his, I wonder if he can feel how hard my nipples are, how much they ache to be in his mouth?

Breaking the kiss, he nudges me backward until my ass hits the edge of a desk. I'm grinning like a fool, my hands slip under his shirt, and move over the perfectly sculpted muscles there. He's ripped, and all I can think about is kissing each and every little bruise, tending to his every want and need.

Before I can get that far though, he's on me, his hands tugging at my shirt, his mouth sucking at my flesh. All I can hear is our heavy pants and my own pulse in my ears. With my shirt off, he pushes my bra straps off my shoulders and removes each breast from its cup before taking a pebbled nipple into his mouth.

My fingers cut through his hair, and I hold his head in place as pleasure flickers deep inside my core.

"Don't stop, don't stop," I pant, wondering if he's going to get me off with nothing but his tongue on my nipple.

"Oh, don't worry, I won't," he smirks around my nipple, releasing it with a loud pop so he can pay the other side the same attention. I can feel how wet I am for him already and know it won't take much to make me come.

"Pants," he orders, reminding me that I've still got them on. While he peppers kisses against my chest, I undo the button on my jeans and slide them down my thighs, kicking them away once they reach my feet.

Oliver breaks away to undo his own bottoms, and within seconds we're both naked. Even in the dim lighting of the room, I can see that his cock is swollen and angry looking. There's a drop of pre-cum on the tip that I crave to lick away.

"My eyes are up here," he says, chuckling, and I can't help but smile.

His hands trail down my body until they reach my hips, once there they come to a stop, he squeezes my flesh before lifting me to place my ass at the edge of the table.

"I have to taste you right now." The urgency in his voice confirms his need, and with a gentle nudge, I'm on my back and lifting my hips for him to pull my panties off. Peeling the silky fabric down my legs, I can't help but grin as he tosses them to the floor and presses my knees to my chest. Leaning in, he gives me one long lick.

"Oh, god..." I mumble at the onslaught of sensations. My

fingers grip on to the edge of the table as he does it all over again, spreading my lips with his fingers. That skilled tongue of his flicks against my swollen clit, and I gush like a waterfall, my legs shaking as he sucks the tiny bud into his mouth. Heat rises in my cheeks, and my entire body warms as lightning rods of pleasure zing up my spine.

"Come for me, come all over my tongue." Oliver's husky voice vibrates through my core, and within seconds I'm falling apart, my hips bucking against his face as he continues licking me, savoring every last drop of my release as if it's a fine wine.

Like a wave, I come crashing back down, my body a liquid mass against the table. Oliver moves from between my legs, coming to stand. There's a carnal look in his eyes, and in that moment, I'm ensnared, trapped in his web, a willing victim to the pleasure he'll bring me.

Through hooded eyes, I watch him stroke his cock. One stroke. Two strokes. My mouth waters. I want him. Need him.

"Please," I whisper, my eyes pleading.

He smirks, "Please, what? Say it. Ask me."

My cheeks flame, but I say it anyway because I'm no longer a shy, naive, virgin. I'm a woman who is loved by three different men. "Please, fuck me."

"Gladly," he growls, gripping on to one hip with a possessiveness that makes me warm inside. Bringing his cock to my wet entrance, he enters me in one thrust, and for one tiny second, all is right in the world. Nothing but us matters. Not what could happen tomorrow, not my father, not anything. There is just us and our joined bodies.

"Fuck me, you're so tight, and warm, and shit, I'm not going to last if you keep squeezing me like that."

All I can do is whimper as he thrusts in and out of me, expelling every last ounce of carnal need that he has. Reaching for him, I let my fingers roam over his perfectly sculpted abs and chest. We're both burning up, on the verge of combusting.

The telltale signs of an orgasm start to snake up my spine. My toes curl, and my chest rises and falls rapidly, and though air fills my lungs, it feels like I can't breathe. Like I'm free-falling out of the sky. It's coming faster than usual, and Oliver must know it because he too starts to thrust harder and faster, bringing me to the edge of the cliff in nothing more than a few strokes.

"I'm coming," I pant, my nails raking across his flesh.

"Yes, come for me. Squeeze me. Milk my cock." His filthy mouth only encourages me, and within seconds I'm shattering like glass that's been squeezed too tightly. My hips buck, and my eyes flutter closed as euphoric pleasure consumes me, wrapping me in a blanket of warmth.

As I'm coming down from my high, floating through the sky like a feather, Oliver starts to fall apart, his movements grow jerky, and I open my eyes to stare up at him, needing to see him come undone.

The brown of his eyes is darker now, and he bites on his bottom lip to stifle a groan. Damn is he sexy. I want to make him feel the same way he made me feel.

"Come inside me, please..." I lick my lips and wait with bated breath for him to fill me with his come.

"Fucking Christ, Harlow," he curses, squeezing my hips with both hands. His hips piston, and all I can feel is him impaling me, breaking me apart to piece me back together again. And I love it. I love him. Three thrusts later and with a groan, I'm pretty sure the entire library heard, he starts to come, his cock pulsing deep inside of me, filling me with his sticky release.

Completely spent and satisfied, he sags against me, his sweaty forehead pressing against mine. Holding him close, I smile, feeling as if I'm on top of the world. I can feel the heat of his release dripping out of me and on to my thighs, his cock still inside of me, still partially hard.

"That was amazing," Oliver pants, "are you okay?" Always so sincere, so caring. That's Oliver, though. He always makes sure that I'm okay. That I came.

"Yes. I'm more than okay," I smile.

"Good, because it's been a while since I came apart that easily," the blistering smile he gives me warms me from the inside out. After a few minutes of lying together, we get up, and he helps me put my clothes back on, minus my panties. He puts those in his pocket as a souvenir.

As I'm sliding my backpack on, he pulls out his phone.

"Shit," he mumbles under his breath. "We're going to be late."

"Ugh, not again," I groan, all while smiling. After what we did, I would say showing up late to class was worth it.

"I won't have time to walk you in to your class if I want to get to my class without being scolded by the professor. So, I'll walk you to the building and then head across the street."

"Okay," I grab onto his hand, and together we walk back down the stairs and into the lower part of the library. As we pass by people, it feels like they are all staring at us, almost like they know what we were doing. Maybe they heard us? But since none of them snicker or smile as we pass, they must not have heard us. I tell myself it's all in my head.

Exiting the library, we hurry across campus and to class. When we reach the sidewalk, we part ways, Oliver pressing a hurried kiss to my lips before seeing me off. As I walk down the sidewalk and enter the building, I give him a little wave and smile before disappearing from view.

When I'm in the building, I realize how late I really am, and instead of walking up the stairs, I basically run, taking two steps at a time.

By the time I reach the top, I have a hard time breathing. *Shit,* I didn't realize how out of shape I am. Maybe I need to start working out.

Taking a few steps, slower this time, I try to regulate my breathing, but it seems to only get worse. This weird feeling that something is wrong overcomes me. I'm not sure what I'm feeling. Not sure what's going on, so I continue onward, hoping that it'll pass. I'm about halfway down the hall when a wave of dizziness crashes into me. It comes out of nowhere and nearly takes me out at the knees. Closing my eyes, I lean against the cold brick wall.

Maybe I just need to do some deep breathing. Forcing air into my lungs, I try and focus on nothing more than my breaths. Sweat beads above my brow, the breathing obviously not helping as my entire body suddenly starts to feel like it's been lit on fire.

Knots of worry tighten in my gut. I don't know what's going on with my body anymore. Another wave of dizziness sends my mind spiraling. I can't even open my eyes without the world spinning around me, and the panic I feel seems to only make it worse.

All at once, my vision goes black, my eyes grow heavier and heavier until I close them again. My mind slowly slipping into unconsciousness. I try to open my eyes again, but I can't. They just won't budge. Faintly, I'm aware of footsteps approaching, and someone asking me if I'm okay. I want to tell them no, that I'm not, but my tongue won't work. All words refuse to be coaxed from my mouth.

Another wave of dizziness overcomes me, and this time when it crashes down, it brings with it the power to snap me in two. Reaching out, I attempt to find something along the wall to support my body. I know I'm going to go down, I can feel it in my gut.

A hand brushes against my arm just as my knees give out and my body folds in half. I'm only partially aware of my body sagging to the floor, my knees slamming against the tile. I don't even feel the impact, there is no pain.

There is nothing but darkness.

12

*D*amnit. I have to stop waking up like this. I know before I even open my eyes where I am. The steady beat of the heart monitor fills my ears, and the smell of antiseptic and bleach tickles my nostrils. *The hospital.* I've put myself in the hospital again. Blinking my eyes open, I'm momentarily blinded by the overhead lights.

My thoughts are fuzzy as I try and recollect what happened.

"Oh, my gosh, she's awake." My mother's voice is the first that I hear, and already I know this is going to be bad. *Why are they here? And where are the guys?*

Nothing serious happened... I just fainted.

"Back up, sweetheart, give her some space." My father orders, and I look up at him, taking note of the dark bags under his eyes and worry in their depths. He looks distraught, but that can't be right. Why should he care about me? He hasn't any other time before now.

"What are you doing here?" I question, squinting my eyes because the light is still blinding me.

My father crosses his arms over his chest, his gaze hardening with each second. "I expected better from you, Harlow. I didn't think you would be this irresponsible, but after everything, I suppose I'm not really surprised."

Whoa, all I did was faint. Maybe I need to take better care of myself. Be less stressed, eat more... I don't know. What I do know is that it's not anything as bad as he's making it out to be.

"Please leave, the hospital was wrong to have called you." I murmur, shaking my head with disappointment. I don't want them here. Neither of them. I'll call one of the Bishops to come and be with me. As I shift against the scratchy sheets, a throbbing starts to pulse behind my eyes. A migraine is forming there, and having my parents here is only making it worse.

"Excuse me, but I am your father even if you don't want me to be, and I have every right as the person who pays for your medical insurance to know what is going on."

I can't help it; my eyes roll to the back of my head on instinct. "Just because you pay my medical bills doesn't mean you're my father. You have to actually act like one to be considered one, and in my eyes, you aren't one, at least to me. Besides, I didn't ask you to pay for anything. Leave the bill and leave me."

A vein bulges in his neck, his cheeks fill with blood, and he starts to look like a red balloon more and more.

"Your mother and I are the only ones here. I don't see your precious Bishop brothers standing next to your bed, checking up on you. Like always, they've done wrong and left the mess for someone else to clean up."

"What are you talking about? There is no mess. I'm fine. I just need to take a little better care of myself. This has nothing to do with them, and the only reason they are not here right now is because they don't know I'm here." My defenses are up. Like always, my father finds a way to make me feel small and insignificant.

A smile like I've never seen before appears on his lips. It's not a kind smile, nor is it really a vicious one. It's more of a, I know something you don't smile, and that leaves my stomach churning, twisting, and knotting.

"Oh, this has everything to do with them. Everything." The way he speaks, with so much disdain, so much vile hate toward the Bishops makes me want to hurt him. How dare he speak about them in such an ill manner. How dare he come here and act like he cares.

"I want you to leave, now," I growl, fisting the sheets to stop myself from getting up and slugging him. He might be my father in the sense of his name being on my birth certificate, but he might as well be a dead-beat. I don't want or need him in my life. All the lies, the secrets, the way he tried to manipulate me. I'll never forget or forgive him for that.

"And I want you to get an abortion."

The room spins around me, my mouth pops open and stays that way as I flounder like a fish out of water. He can't mean… No, it's not possible. How? I'm on birth control. He's lying. He has to be.

"What… what are you talking about?" I ask, finally finding the courage to speak. My voice wavers between barely restrained panic and fear.

"Do you even know which one of them is the father? Wait, don't answer that. It doesn't matter who the father is. You'll be getting an abortion either way."

"I'm pregnant?" I say the words out loud as if I didn't

already put the pieces together. Of course, I'm pregnant. How did I not see this before?

"Not for much longer," my father chides, looking down at me like I'm a disappointment to the world. Well, likewise, dearest dad.

"It's a good thing you don't have a say in it, isn't it? Now leave. I never asked for you to be here, and I won't let you dictate any more of my life!" I yell, gathering up every ounce of strength I have to sit up a little taller. Maybe he could push me around before, make me be his little puppet, but not anymore.

I'm about to yell, to tell them to get the hell out again when someone knocks on the door, interrupting my little outburst.

"Come in," my mother answers before I can make a sound. I watch the door as the unknown person pushes it open. Every fiber in my body hoping and praying that one of the guys is on the other side of that door. But when the door swings open all the way, all I'm left with is more disappointment.

Even though it's someone I know, it's not one of the Bishops like I had hoped it would be. My stomach drops, and I feel like I might throw up as I watch Matt leisurely walk into the room. His gaze sweeps over the room before coming to rest on me. He doesn't even look like he cares. All over again, I'm reminded of how I'm nothing but a pawn to my father.

"Matt, thank you so much for coming," my father greets him, making it sound more like a business arrangement.

"No problem. How are you feeling, Harlow?" he asks, coming to stand beside the bed.

"Terrible, and you being here doesn't help," I snap at

him. Not caring how rude I must sound. The last thing I want is to be surrounded by these people that don't care if I'm happy or not, people that only want me to play a part in their shitty story.

"Ouch," Matt smirks. He's clearly not offended by my words.

"Be nice," my mother scolds, and I barely restrain the growl as my lip curls with anger. "We're going to give you two a moment. Don't mess this up, Harlow. This might be your last chance to save yourself from complete destruction. Make the right choice, so that we don't have to make it for you."

My last chance? What the hell is that supposed to mean?

My parents leave the room, and Matt grabs a chair dragging it over to the bed. It scratches against the floor loudly, but he doesn't seem to care. He takes a seat, the chair creaking under his weight. He's only a foot away from me now, and I shiver at the thought of him being this close, especially after the way he treated me the last time I saw him.

Giving me a boyish grin, he says, "So, I heard you got knocked up by one of those Bishop brothers."

"I don't see how this is your business."

Matt shrugs, "Your dad wants you to get rid of the baby, but I've got a better idea. A way that will allow you to keep it. Since the beginning, I've told you I was here to help."

I'd laugh if I didn't already have a headache the size of Texas, and it didn't hurt to move. "Ha, doubtful. You've never wanted to help me. You're a disgusting, selfish prick, and I want you to leave and never come back."

What I have to say doesn't matter to him. I know this. I've known it all along. Maybe I had hoped he would be different, that he would become a friend to me. That turned out to be nothing but a lie too.

Crossing his arms over his chest, he stares me down, his gaze hardening. "I'm being very generous to you and your family, Harlow. I'm still willing to marry you. I don't mind that you're having a baby, in fact, it's one less thing I have to do." He winks at me, and I gag, the thought… it makes me want to barf all over the floor.

"No one has to know who the real father is. I'm willing to raise it as my own, give it, and you a home, a life. I'll protect you, ensure that you're happy and healthy."

I can't believe him. Does he even hear himself?

"You're a lunatic if you think I'm going to go along with this. I'll never marry you. With or without this baby. It's not happening," I snarl. I have this impulse to scratch his eyes out, to do whatever I can to get him out of this room and away from me. I don't need him or my parents. I can do this all on my own.

Matt chuckles a humorless laugh, "You are the crazy one. If you don't do this, your father will make you get an abortion. He's not going to let you have this baby any other way." He pauses, and I'm hoping he'll shut the hell up and get out, but he doesn't. Instead, he opens his mouth again. "Do you know what kind of embarrassment this would be to him? A baby with his sworn enemy's son? Hell, you don't even know who the father is."

"I don't care. I don't care what any of you think or say…" I whisper, all the emotions inside of me swirling together.

He unfolds his arms and runs a hand through his hair, before exhaling a deep breath, "Look, he's not going to let you leave this hospital with that baby inside of you. Not unless you agree to marry me. The abortion will happen today, you have no say."

"He can't do that! He wouldn't..." I argue, but even as the words leave my mouth, I know the truth is, he would. He is probably paying this hospital half a fortune to do this without my consent, or maybe he is just threatening them with whatever sick thing he can come up with. The lump in my throat thickens as I weigh my options. It feels like all hope is lost.

"I'm just trying to help," Matt tells me, and anger overwrites my fear momentarily.

"Like you were trying to *help* me the last time I saw you. When you threatened me?"

He shrugs like it's no big deal at all, but his eyes hold his emotions inside. Like a glass house, Matt is the type of person that will crack, snap, shatter if you hit him enough times.

"I admit, I was drunk and out of line. I'll try not to let it happen again."

"You'll try?" I snort. "Well, at least you are honest."

"I try to be, but that doesn't mean I don't make mistakes. In all seriousness, you don't know what your father is willing to do. You don't know the lengths he'll go to get what he wants. I'm your best choice right now. Actually, I'm your only choice." Only then does the reality of this all hit me. I'm pregnant. I'm carrying a child inside me, and my father wants to kill it. Fear settles deep inside my bones, and I know I need to do everything I can to save the life inside of me, but marrying Matt can't be the answer.

"You might be the lesser of two evils, but that doesn't mean I will just marry you," I whisper. "I'm in love with someone else." A coldness fills the room, and dread clings to my bones. "If you really wanted to help me, you would give me your phone and let me make a call. You would help me get out of here."

Matt blows out a frustrated breath, "And how would that benefit me? Didn't you listen to anything I've said to you? Going against your father never ends well, that doesn't exclude me. If I go against him, if I try and save you, he'll retaliate, and I can't afford that. He would—"

A knock on the door interrupts Matt mid-sentence, and we both turn toward it.

"We need a few more minutes," I yell before the door can open.

"Okay, take your time," my father's muffled voice filters through the door, and even from here, I can hear the triumphant tone in his voice. He already assumes that he's won. He thinks I'm agreeing to Matt's proposal. The joke's on him though. I'll die before I do a single thing, he wants me to.

Instead, I know I'm going to have to convince Matt in whatever way I can.

"Matt, please help me. Really *help* me. Don't let him do this. Don't let them kill my baby, please..." I don't care that I'm begging or how desperate I might sound. I'll get on my knees if that's what gets him to help me.

For the first time, I see real empathy reflecting back at me. He gets up from the chair and steps really close, taking my hand into his.

"I won't let him kill the baby, okay." He lowers his voice and leans into me. "I'll tell him that I want you pregnant, but you have to agree to marry me now, even if it's only to buy yourself time. I won't be able to help you contact your boyfriends, and if they don't show up on their own, then you might have to marry me, after all. I can't go against your father."

"Okay, thank you..." I can't believe what I'm about to say next, but like he said, right now, he is my best bet. "Will you stay here with me. I don't want to be alone with my parents."

He nods and sits back down, just as someone knocks on the door once more.

"You can come in now," I call out, and the door opens. My parents walk in, my father has a smug grin on his face, and it takes everything inside of me to bite my tongue.

"Did you two come to an agreement?" he asks even though I know for a fact that he already knows.

"I'll marry Matt," I grit out. That sinister grin on my father's face only grows.

"And I'm okay with her having the baby," Matt announces. "No one needs to know that I'm not the father."

"Great," my mom cheers and claps her hands together. "I'm so excited. The wedding is back on then."

I force a smile and nod slightly, hoping with all my heart that the guys find me before it's too late because if they don't... I don't even want to think of the mess that will come when all the pieces fall.

13

My parents left after our talk yesterday, and even though I felt fine after they pumped some fluids in me, the doc insisted on keeping me overnight for observation. Matt ended up staying with me in the hospital the whole night, sleeping on a pull out chair the nurse brought in. Part of me is glad that he is here, and I'm not alone with my father's goons who are posted outside my door. But there is another part of me that has a hard time trusting Matt, considering the way he's treated me in the past.

I'm trying to hold on to the fact that he has never lied to me... at least, not that I know of. Assuming he is telling me the truth, he won't let anything happen to the baby and me, and right now, that is the most important thing. As much as I love the Bishop brothers, I already love the life growing inside of me just as fiercely, maybe even more.

After breakfast, one of the nurses comes in to take my tray. Smiling at me sweetly, she asks, "Is there anything else you need this morning?"

"Actually, I could use a little help going to the bathroom. The IV makes it hard to get around," I say, glancing over at Matt, who frowns at me. I'm sure he knows what I'm up to, but to my relief, he doesn't say anything when the nurse helps me out of bed and into the bathroom. As soon as she closes the door behind us, I turn around and look at her.

"Please, I need your help," I whisper. "I'm here against my will. I need to make a phone call. Can I please use your cell phone?"

I see the brief shock in her eyes before she lowers her gaze to the ground. "I'm sorry. I can't help you." Her apology sounds genuine, and I know my father must have threatened the staff here. "I am sorry. Really."

"It's okay, I know you are," I say in defeat.

"Do you need help to use the bathroom?"

"No, not really…" As soon as I say the words, she scurries out of the room, whispering another *sorry* on her way out.

I use the toilet on my own before brushing my teeth and washing my face. Every move I make is on autopilot, my mind too busy being worried and scared about what's to come.

When I get back into the room, Matt is still sitting in the chair, only now he's reclined it and his feet are propped up.

"I'm guessing she didn't go for it?"

"My father must have really freaked her out. She couldn't get away fast enough after I asked to use her phone."

"You don't give up easily, I'll give you that. You think after three times, you would stop trying," Matt says, tucking a blanket over himself. "I'm taking a nap; I hardly got any sleep last night with you snoring so loudly."

"I do not snore!"

"Whatever you have to tell yourself, princess," Matt chuckles, closing his eyes.

I crawl back into my bed, careful not to tug on the needle still sticking inside my arm. Turning on the TV, I flip through the channels, landing on some cooking show. I don't really care about it, but I need something to take my mind off the reality I am in.

After twenty minutes, Matt starts to snore softly, letting me know he is asleep. I keep glancing at the door, wondering if my father's guards are still there or if they left. After five minutes of inner dialogue, I talk myself into trying to leave.

Carefully, I remove the tape around the IV in my arm before pulling out the needle slowly. Blood starts to puddle on my skin, and I quickly take my bed sheet and press it onto the spot until it stops bleeding.

Trying to not make any noise, I slowly slide out of my bed and tiptoe toward the door on sock covered feet. I'm in my own clothes, which my mother brought me last night, but I don't have any shoes. I don't have to get far, anyway, only far enough to find someone who isn't on my father's payroll or has been threatened by him.

I'm almost at the door, my hand already reaching for the doorknob when I freeze. Holding my breath, I listen to a man's voice right outside my door. A voice I know all too well.

My father. Shit.

His voice is coming closer, and I hurry back into bed with my heart pounding in my chest. I barely manage to hop back in and pull the blanket over my arm, before the door opens and my father walks in without knocking.

"Harlow," he greets me mechanically, and I sit up straight

in bed. Matt startles awake at my father's entrance, seeming just as surprised as I am to see him here.

"What do you want from me now?"

"I actually came to talk to Matt," he scowls at me. "However, I would appreciate it if you could stop harassing your nurses to use their phones."

God, I want to throw something at him. Preferable something heavy.

"Matt, a word outside."

"Sure," Matt answers, getting up from his chair, he gives me a look that says *behave* on his way out.

You behave yourself. I yell after him in my head. The door closes, leaving me all alone in the room. I throw the blanket back, jump up and tiptoe back to the door, pressing my ear to the wood so I can hear better.

"Telling her you wanted the baby was stupid, Matt," My father growls. "I don't want her to have that child. If she wants a baby so badly, you're gonna have to do it, I can't watch a child of *theirs* grow up under my nose," my father spits. "We are going through with the abortion. I don't care what she wants. If she didn't want this to happen, then maybe she should've kept her legs closed."

Fear trickles down my spine. *No! He can't!* There is no way I'll let him do this, and if he does, then I'll never forgive him.

Matt's voice cuts through, "I'm worried about her, and I don't think it's a good idea to do this. Harlow and I are in a good place now. She's just started to warm up to me, and doing this would mess everything I've worked toward. You don't have to do this. I'll raise the baby as my own. No one has to know who the father is, and no one would dare question my family and me."

"I'll know, and that's all that matters! And I don't care about *feelings*. I care about my reputation, and what this will do to me, and so should you. It's already been decided. We're going through with this. End of story." My dad barks, and I stagger back.

The door opens a moment later, my father and Matt appearing in front of me with three nurses right behind them. Two females and one male. Shaking my head profusely, I watch Matt's face contort into a mixture of both sorrow and shame.

He can stop this. I know he can, so why isn't he?

"No, you can't do this!" I scream and take a few steps back, only to hit the wall. I'm trapped. There is no place to go. "Please," I beg, but no one listens. Their faces are blank like they're not even here mentally.

The male nurse grabs one of my arms so tightly, I know there will be bruises. Still, I struggle, trying my best to fight them off. I won't go down without a fight.

"Please don't do this," I look to my father who is staring at me with nothing more than disappointment in his eyes. He's supposed to be my father. He's supposed to care about me. How could he do this? To me? To his unborn grandchild, and all because of a last name?

"You brought this on yourself, Harlow," my father says, his voice clipped.

Tears sting my eyes, and I wince when the female nurse grabs on to my other arm, her fingers biting into my flesh with the same harshness.

It's then that I spot the syringe in the third nurse's hand. *No. No.* I shake my head, wishing that this was nothing but a bad dream.

Subdued against the wall, I watch helplessly as the

needle pierces through my skin, pain followed by a cold tingling sensation spreads through my veins. "Stop!" I scream as loud as I can, my throat throbbing.

Even with the syringe empty and the fact that I've given up fighting, the nurses still hold on to me like I'm going to bolt for the door, then again, if they released me, I would do just that.

"Okay, that's enough. Let her go," Matt growls the look in his eyes is murderous, and immediately the hands on me disappear, but I can still feel them. Still, feel the pain. Still, feel the needle in my arm.

My body starts to sag toward the floor like goop, but Matt steps in and grabs me at the last minute. His arms come around my waist, supporting most of my weight, and I can't help but seek his comfort in that moment.

He's the only thing I have right now, the only person who cares if I live or die. And as badly as I want to hate him, in this moment, I can't bring myself to. We're both pawns in this war. Burying my face into his chest, I start to cry. Sobbing uncontrollably, I can feel the medication they gave me kicking in. My limbs are getting heavier, and my mind fuzzier by the second.

"You promised..." I whimper, clutching on to his shirt. A warmth courses through me, my cheeks heat, and my whole body starts to tingle. All the discomfort in my body starts to fade.

"I know," Matt whispers back. I've lost all hope now. I'm going to lose this baby; this tiny little human is going to be taken from me before I even get the chance to tell the guys about it. Leaning down, he nuzzles his face into my hair. "I need you to trust me, okay. I won't let this happen. I'll find a way to fix this."

Shaking my head, I try to speak, but my tongue feels heavy.

I want to tell him that I wish I could believe him. That I want to believe him and his words so badly, but I can't. I can't trust anyone. Still, a part of me hangs on to the hope that maybe, just maybe he won't let me down this time. But how? How can he help me? How can he stop this from happening? He said so himself, he won't go against my father. No one will. Not the hospital staff, not Matt, not the Bishops. I'm doomed. My child will die, and there is nothing I can do about it. Spots form over my vision, and no matter how much I try to hang on to that last shred of light, it slowly dims out, getting lighter and lighter.

My last thought before everything goes black is that I hope the guys will forgive me for this. Forgive me for failing to protect our child.

∞

When I wake up, the same heaviness I felt earlier remains in my limbs, and the fuzziness engulfing my mind only increases. I feel like my brain has been run through a blender and has been poured back into my skull, but even with my head being in utter disarray, I remember what happened before I passed out.

The pain in my chest only gets more prominent, the emptiness expanding and leaving a hollow space behind.

I pry my eyes open, just to squeeze them shut again when I see my father standing at the end of the bed. I thought I hated him before, but the hatred I feel for him has grown into a colossal amount over the last few hours. I can't put into words how much I despise my father for doing this, how much I loathe him for taking this child from me... for killing the life inside of me.

I never considered myself a violent person before, but if I had the strength to do so now, I would kill him. If I never again see this man who called himself my father, I would be a happier person... that is if I can ever find happiness after what was done to me.

"I'll leave you to deal with this," my father's voice cuts through the fog surrounding my head like clouds surround the top of a mountain. "Since you two seem to get along so great now," he continues, and for a moment, I don't understand who he is talking to.

"We *did* get along, but after what you did to her, she is never going to trust me again," Matt barks.

"Trust is overrated. There are other ways to keep people in line. More effective ways," my father declares. I can hear him turn, his expensive leather shoes making a squeaking sound against the hospital floor as he does. I listen to each of his steps as he is leaving the room. The door opening and closing, leaving me alone with the man who promised to keep my child and me safe.

I didn't realize how cold I was until a large warm hand comes down to rest on my icy cold fingers. Even though the warmth feels good on my frozen skin, I pull my hand away at once, not wanting to feel an ounce of relief and comfort. Because I don't deserve either one. I deserve to be cold, alone, and in pain after I failed... I failed everybody I loved.

"Harlow," Matt whispers as he tries to capture my hand once more. Again, I pull away, and when he tries to touch my cheek, I turn my face away as well.

"Don't touch me," I croak, barely able to make the words come out at all.

"Harlow, listen to me..." Matt pleads with me, but all I do is shake my head. "Open your eyes and look at me."

"No," I sob, realizing I'm already crying again. Tears roll down my cheeks, leaving cold tracks behind. "Leave..."

"I won't leave you here," Matt tells me as he places a hand on my stomach. My eyes fly open in shock, and a wave of all-consuming anger engulfs me. How dare he touch me there... how dare he touch me at all?

Like a wild fury, I start shoving at his arm, slapping, scratching, and hitting him wherever I can, letting out all the burning anger inside of me.

"I said, don't fucking touch me! I hate you!"

Matt catches my flailing arms mid-air, wrapping his fingers around my already sore wrists and pinning them next to my body.

"Listen, Harlow!" Matt whisper yells. "Just listen! It didn't happen, okay?"

It didn't happen? What is that supposed to mean? Is he telling me to just forget about it? Forget what he and my father did to me?

"Do you feel any pain?" he asks next. "Any discomfort?"

Other than the suffocating ache in my chest, he means? "Yes, my whole damn body hurts."

"But your stomach doesn't hurt, does it?"

I blink some of the tears away, trying to look at his face, and make sense of what he's trying to tell me. A smile tucks on his lips, and when I finally stop fighting him, he released my wrists. No, now that I'm concentrating on feeling each part of my body, I realize that he is right. My lower abdomen doesn't hurt, and there is no soreness between my legs. If I'd had an abortion, wouldn't I feel both?

"The baby?"

"Still inside of you," Matt says. "I paid off the doctor. He just pretended to do the abortion. The baby is fine." I watch his face carefully, looking for any indication that he is lying, but his eyes are genuine, his smile is kind, and his voice is gentle.

"I'm... I'm still pregnant?" I ask again, needing to confirm, even though deep inside, I already know the answer.

"Yes, you are still pregnant, and now with your dad off your back, you should be able to stay that way too."

I tuck my arm under the blanket to put my hand on my still flat stomach, rubbing the skin there like the baby could somehow feel it. "Why? Why did you help me?"

"I told you I would. What your dad did was unforgivable, and I couldn't watch him go through with it. He went too far, even for my standards, and I'm a pretty big asshole."

I used to think so too. I thought Matt was a huge jerk, and maybe he still is by other standards, but after he risked going against my father to help me, I can't feel anything but gratitude toward him.

"So, what now? He is going to find out eventually."

"Honestly, I haven't thought that far ahead. I don't know how to get you out of here without your father knowing I helped you."

"Thank you, really, thank you, I don't know how I can ever repay you for what you did. It's not your fault that my father is this way, and I'm not your responsibility. I'm no one's responsibility. Not even the Bishops. I will get out of this on my own. I will fight my father. I won't let him control me and the people around me anymore. I won't let him continue using you, or anyone else for that matter. I'm going to be the one to put an end to his reign."

"This is dangerous, Harlow, going against your father. He has resources, money, people." Matt sounds almost afraid, and that strikes something inside of me. Even the most powerful of people have a weakness, and while my father has all the things he needs to destroy me, I have the determination needed to fight back.

I'm done being afraid. Done worrying about what might happen next. If I don't, at least try to fight him, I'll never escape. I'll never really be free.

"I can't stay here, Matt, I can't stay with you, you know that. Not only because of the baby, but because of my father. I won't be stuck under his thumb. I won't be married off or tossed away like garbage."

Matt scrubs a hand down his face in frustration, and a little piece of my heart feels bad for putting him in this situation.

"I won't force you to do anything, and I'll do what I can to help you, but I can't make any promises," he finally says.

"That's all I'm asking for. That's all I need. I'll do the rest on my own."

Now all I need to do is come up with a plan.

14

Neither one of my parents came back to the hospital today, and I am more than happy they didn't. I don't think I could stand to be in the same room with either one of them right now.

"Are you sure you're going to be okay on your own?" Matt asks for the third, and hopefully, final time.

"Yes, I promise. They need you at that meeting so go to work. I've held up enough of your time." The truth is, even though I now value Matt's company, I want him to leave. I don't want my father to think that he helped me escape. The last thing I want is anyone else to get hurt.

"I'll only be a few hours, then I'll come back and pick you up. Your father has reluctantly agreed on you staying with me," Matt says while slipping his arms into his jacket.

"Okay..." I try to force a smile when he glances my way, but I don't think it's very convincing.

"You know, your dad has two guards posted outside that door at all times?" Matt sighs. Of course, he's figured it out. He's intuitive like that. I'm glad he's not trying to stop me.

"I know. I mean, I figured. Thanks for the heads up."

"Be careful, Harlow," Matt warns, but it's not the threatening kind of warning, is more like the concerned kind of warning. He stops at the door, his hand already resting on the doorknob when he turns around to look at me one more time.

"Good luck," he says, just loud enough for me to hear it.

"Goodbye, Matt," I murmur, not sure when or even if I'll see him again.

The door closes, and I'm left in the large empty hospital room on my own. Loneliness and dejection creep up on me, like shadows in the night, trying to pull me into darkness. I try not to let them get to me, knowing that this is only a momentary state. I am not really alone, not as long as I have people who love me out there waiting for me, probably worried sick about me.

I wait about twenty minutes before I start moving. This is probably long enough for no one to suspect Matt helped me in any way. Grabbing my empty food tray, I stick it under my armpit and grab two boxes of orange juice, that I saved from breakfast. Opening them up carefully, I walk to the door, holding them in one hand, and grabbing the shiny silver doorknob with the other.

My pulse is racing, and my knees are shaking, but my mind is sharp as a blade. There might be some truck-sized men on the other side of this door, but my determination to leave this place is stronger than any two-hundred-pound man.

Sucking in a deep breath, I let the plan run through my head one final time.

Then, I open the door.

I step outside and find two guys sitting on the other side

of the corridor looking up at me simultaneously. "I need a nurse right now, this juice is bad," I complain like I'm an angry customer in a restaurant, and they are the managers.

"Go back in there," one of them growls at me, not hiding his annoyance at my request.

Instead of following his orders, I grab on to the tray under my arm and throw it at his head as hard as I can. Like I had hoped, I catch both of them completely by surprise. With the tray flying through the air and both of them distracted, I bolt.

As I sprint down the hall, I drop the two boxes of juice behind me.

"You fucking brat!" One of them yells after me.

Concentrating on making my legs move as fast as I can and nothing more, I continue forward. When I hear what sounds like someone slipping, followed by a loud thud, and a string of curse words, I know my plan has worked.

I can't help but smile at this small triumph, even though I know damn well that I'm not safe yet. My sock covered feet pound against the hospital floor as I let the bright red EXIT signs guide me to freedom.

Since I don't know who my father has paid off in this place, I decide against stopping for anything or anyone until I'm outside. I pass a few shocked and confused nurses and patients, but I don't stop. I continue running through the blinding white hospital hallways like a madwoman on a mission because I am.

After what seems like an eternity of running through the maze of halls, I finally make it to a pair of sliding glass doors. Through them, I can see a parking lot, cars, people... *freedom.*

I'm so close to escaping, so close to being free.

Creeping toward the doors, I finally glance behind me to see if I'm being trailed. When I find no one, my shoulders almost sag with relief. The sliding doors open, and I dart through them. Fresh air caresses my skin, and sunlight warms my face as I take my first steps outside. I want to stand there for a moment; to catch my breath and enjoy these feelings coursing through me, but I know I need to keep moving. I need to get as far away from here as I can. I'm not safe, not until I'm back with the brothers.

Ignoring the throbbing of my shoe-less feet with each bang against the concrete, I race toward the main road. Not wanting to waste any time, I cut the corner sharply, too sharply it seems, because as soon as I round the edge of the wall, my body comes crashing into another person. The impact knocks the air from my lungs, and if the person wasn't holding on to me, I'd probably have fallen on my ass.

Before I even look up from the guy's chest, I know who it is. The familiar smell of forest and rain tickles my nostrils, and like a small child, I wrap my arms around his middle and bury my face into his chest.

"Fuck, Harlow," he croaks into my hair. His arms come around me, enclosing me in a cocoon. "We need to get out of here."

I pull away from him, even though my body objects, wanting to stay here with him. Just like this, in a perfect little bubble where no one can hurt us.

Taking my hand in his, Sullivan starts to pull me away, but before we even make the first step, a car comes barreling toward us. Tires squeal against the asphalt as it comes to a sudden halt. My gaze widens when I spot Oliver in the front seat. My eyes catching sight of Banks running toward us from the other side of the road.

Sullivan pulls the door open, helping me into the back seat, just as Banks approaches from the other side, climbing into the passenger seat up front.

As soon as we are all in the car, Oliver presses his foot to the pedal, and we speed off. The acceleration pushes me into the leather seats as relief, and endless happiness engulfs me. I'm safe now.

"Are you okay?" Banks asks, turning around in his seat.

Sullivan hasn't stopped touching me. Running his hands all over me as if he was checking for any wounds.

"I'm okay, just so glad to see you. How... how did you find me?"

"Matt called us when he left the hospital," Oliver explains. "He told us where you were and that you were probably going to make a run for it."

"He did?" I ask, instantly, worry starts coating my insides. If anyone finds out what he did, my father will crucify him.

"We got here as fast as we could," Banks says breathlessly. "We've been so fucking worried; we've been looking everywhere for you."

"I promise, I'm fine. I just can't believe I'm finally out of that hospital, and I can't believe Matt called you. But, of course, I'm glad he did. I'm just worried about at what cost." Pushing the thought away, I ask something else that's on my mind. "Did he tell you anything else?"

"That's all he said when he called," Sullivan confirms before questioning me frantically. "What is it? Are you hurt? Did someone hurt you?"

"No, no. I told you, I'm fine. It's nothing bad. I mean, at least I hope you don't feel like it's a bad thing. I don't think it's a bad thing. I guess we never talked about it..." I keep rambling on nervously.

"Harlow," Banks cuts me off. "Out with it."

Clearing my throat, I say, "I'm pregnant."

Dead silence fills the car, and as it stretches on, I start to get seriously worried. Maybe they are not as happy as I am about a baby? Glancing over to Sullivan, I find him staring at me, his eye impossibly wide, his face pale, and his lips slightly parted.

"Say something," I whisper.

Sullivan blinks, almost like my voice has snapped him out of some trance. "You're pregnant?" he finally asks. "Like you are having, kind of, a baby, pregnant?"

"Erm, is there another kind of pregnant?"

Banks turns once more, so I can see his face again. To my relief, there is a huge grin spread across his lips. "We're having a baby?" he asks, his voice filled with happiness and excitement.

"Yeah, we are."

When I glance back over to Sullivan, he seems to have composed himself as well. The shock has left his face, and the corners of his lips tug upward into a dazzling smile.

Two down, one to go.

"Oliver?" I ask tentatively. "How do you feel about this?"

"I-I'm just shocked. I mean, I thought you were on the pill?" Oliver starts but stopping himself right away. "Shit, that came out wrong. Sorry, I'm not saying it's your fault or anything. Not saying it's anyone's fault...Ugh, that came out wrong too."

"Dude, just stop talking," Banks scolds his brother. "For now, just shove your foot in your mouth, will you?"

I try my best not to frown. For some reason, I thought Oliver would be the happiest with having a baby, considering he is the oldest. Apparently, I was wrong. I'm not angry or anything, and I know this was unplanned and not ideal, but this is what happens when people have sex.

Sometimes they get pregnant even while on the pill. Everybody knows this, so why is he acting like this now? Why is he so unhappy?

The whirlwind of emotions leaves me utterly confused. I'm happy to be out of the hospital and away from my parents. I'm relieved to see the guys, but I'm heartbroken and scared seeing Oliver's reaction. Does he really not want this baby? I can't imagine he would ever tell me to get rid of it, but his response isn't anything like I thought it would be.

"Hey," Sullivan reaches over and cradles my face with his hand. His touch is warm, and instantly, I lean into his touch like a kitten who wants to be petted. "Everything is going to be okay. We're not going anywhere."

He can't possibly assure me that it will be. Still, I take comfort in his promise.

"Now, please tell us what the hell happen? How did Matt end up helping you?"

I take a deep breath before explaining the whole story. Just when I'm done, we pull up to the house. Oliver kills the engine once we reach the end of the driveway and we all climb out of the car. Sullivan's hand never leaves my body as he helps me every step of the way. Like he is scared that I'm going to disappear again.

Right now, I need his touch. I need it like I need my next breath. I want him to touch me more. I want him to wrap his arms around me and never let me go again. I want to curl up in bed with all three of them, having them surround me like a protective wall.

On the way inside the house, Banks comes up to my side, while Oliver unlocks the door.

"Are you hungry, thirsty, tired?" he questions as he takes my hand into his.

"I'm fine. A little tired, but definitely not hungry. They did feed me pretty well in that hospital. Since it was a private facility, they actually had restaurant-quality food."

"I guess that's the only good thing about the place." I couldn't agree more. I hated the place and hated that my father had tried to hurt my unborn baby there.

Walking inside, Banks closes the door behind him, twisting all the locks into place. Oliver leads the way into the living room, and the rest of us follow. Once we are all situated on the couch, I direct all my attention to Oliver. I can't let this hang in the air between us. I need to know what he's thinking. If he's okay with the baby.

"Is me being pregnant that bad? Do you not want this... us?" My voice cracks at the end, emotions overtaking my ability to speak evenly.

Oliver's angelic face falls. "I'm sorry, Harlow. I'm still trying to wrap my head around it. You... us, having a child together. The thought of it has my heart bursting with happiness. I just..." he trails off, running his fingers through his thick brown hair. I can feel his frustration from where he is sitting.

"What's the problem? If you're happy, then why do you seem so frustrated? Why do you seem so *unhappy?*" Oliver's gaze clashes with mine, and everything around us fades away.

"We can barely protect you, Harlow. Every time we think you are safe, there seems to be another threat lurking in the shadows, ready to take you away from us." The sadness that radiates out of him is stifling. "Do you have any idea what the last few days have been like for us? Now with you being pregnant, it's only going to get worse. It's like we can never catch a break."

"Oh, Oliver," I sigh in relief. Getting up from where I'm sitting, I crawl into his lap, wrapping my arms around his neck. He welcomes me into his arms, doing the same, his giant hands rub gently up and down my back while he peppers kisses all over my face. He does want the baby; he's just scared of something happening to us.

"Oliver does have a point," Banks mumbles after a while. "There is something we need to tell you. Another thing that we have to protect you against."

Twisting around in Oliver's lap, I look up between all three of them, waiting for one of them to continue. When they don't, I open my mouth to speak.

"What is it?"

Sullivan gives me a sad look. "The police called earlier today... to warn us," Sullivan explains, "Shelby escaped from the psych ward last night."

It's a good thing I'm sitting because if I wasn't, I would be on the floor right now.

"What? What do you mean she *escaped*?" How can she escape? She was supposed to be locked up." This is bad, so bad. Already, I can feel the pressure of what this means settling on my shoulders. She escaped, she's out, free, doing god knows what. Before I know what I'm doing, my hands come to rest on my stomach, cradling my imaginary bump. There is so much more at stake now, so much more than just protecting me.

All of Oliver's worries and fears, they come crashing into me then.

He's right, as sad as it is, he is right. I can barely protect myself. How am I going to protect this child?

15

The weight of the world seems to sit on my shoulders. I do the basics; showering, eating, and trying to sleep. Days pass, and once again, I find I'm stuck in this house, hiding from the world. Oliver and Sullivan leave for class, while Banks stays behind with me. We all agreed me returning to classes again was all but pointing a bright red arrow at where I was. Shelby could easily get to me if she wanted to.

And I suppose she could get to me here too if she really wanted.

"Please stop frowning, your sad face makes me sad." Banks pouts.

That makes me smile, "It's hard to be happy when it feels like everything is falling apart. I thought she was put away forever." I drop my gaze to my hands, "I thought we were safe. Now it feels like all we were doing was lying in wait."

Banks' hands cover my own, and he sits down on the cushion beside me. "All we can do is wait for the police to find her, and right now, no one knows where she is. Maybe she ran away? Maybe she decided hurting you wasn't really what she wanted after all?"

"You really think she would escape just to be free, and not to track me down and hurt me more?" I lift my gaze and stare at him in disbelief. If he says yes, I'm going to be forced to smack some sense into him.

"No, but I can only hope. The last thing I want is for her to try and come after you."

"Same. All I want is for all the threats, all the stress to go away." Pausing, I can feel the emotions swirling inside me, brewing just like a thunderstorm does. "I'm scared, and not just for me but the baby too. What if she finds me? What if she hurts the baby?"

I'm spiraling out of control, my thoughts headed into a dark and dangerous place.

"Stop, she isn't going to touch you or the baby, and nothing is going to happen to either of you, not if I have anything to say about it." Banks' soft tone is meant to reassure me, it's meant to calm me, but nothing will stop me from worrying, nothing but knowing that she is behind bars where she really belongs.

The buzzing of my cell phone against the coffee table has me lurching toward the device. I take it into my hands and stare at the name flashing across the screen. It's my stepmom. What could she possibly want?

My finger hovers over the green answer key, but a head shake from Banks helps me make my decision. Talking to her isn't going to help me any, not when all she's going to do is hurt me more with her hateful words and tell me how horrible I am for running away. For hurting Matt.

"I don't know what she wants, but I can tell you that it's nothing good. If she has something to say, she'll leave a voicemail." Banks says. Moving from the couch and heading for the kitchen. "Are you hungry? You have to be. I know if I were pregnant, I would be eating the house down."

"You eat the house down normally, so what's the difference?" I giggle.

Banks cocks his head to the side as he opens the fridge and inspects its contents, "I suppose there isn't a difference. Maybe I would eat twice as much then? Or four times as much since I technically eat for two already?"

My phone beeps, letting me know that my stepmom has left a voicemail, and because I'm curious, I grab the device, going to the voicemail before bringing it to my ear.

"Hi, sweetie, it's me. I just wanted to call and make sure you were okay. We got word that Shelby escaped the psych ward, and I wanted to warn you and make sure that you were safe. I know that we ended things badly at the hospital, but your father and I just want the best for you. We have the police searching for Shelby and will do everything we can to protect you. We love you. Call me or your father if you need anything."

The voicemail ends, and I'm left with my mouth hanging open. How can she act so normal after everything that happened at the hospital? How can they act like they give one single fuck what happens to me?

"I told you nothing good would come from that woman," Banks interrupts my thoughts.

"She claims they want to warn me about Shelby, and that they're working with the police to catch her. They'll do everything they can to protect me."

Banks rolls his bright blue eyes, pulling stuff out to make some sandwiches, "Pfft, protect you from what? They're the reason that all of this happened. Your father and Shelby are perfect for each other, and your stepmom is a gold-digging bitch. They all should be in that mental hospital together."

He's not wrong.

"All I want is for everything to end, for my father to leave me alone, and let me be happy, and for Shelby to get what she deserves."

"It'll happen. We'll make sure of it. No one is going to hurt you anymore. You and that baby are the most important things to us, and I'll be damned if I stand by and let people hurt you again."

My heart decides to do that stupid pitter-patter thing in my chest, and I can't help but smile, my lips turning up at the sides. It feels foreign like I shouldn't be doing it, but I want to smile. I want to be happy.

Together Banks and I eat an early lunch. Afterward, we chill on the couch for a little while, where he cradles my belly and talks in a baby voice to it. I laugh so hard that my eyes tear up. For a few hours, I forget about the heartache that is behind us, all the hurdles we'll have to get over in the future, and all the uncertainties we'll have to face.

At the time, I didn't know that this was going to be the calm before the storm. A moment of blissful happiness before everything comes crashing down on me. Before, my life took a turn for the worst.

"I think I'm going to take a nap," I yawn after we've been lying still for a while.

"Go ahead, I'll clean up the dishes from earlier and maybe join you in a little bit."

"Alright, I'll try and wait up for you," I tell him and plant a quick kiss on his very kissable lips. I want to linger there longer, but I know if I do, I'll never get to take a nap, and lately, that's all I've wanted to do. Sleep, and eat, and sleep some more.

Walking into my bedroom, I realize that I don't even need to change clothes since I stayed in my PJs all day. I slip into my bed, the one I rarely sleep in. I usually spend the night in one of the guys' rooms, but they still wanted me to have my own room.

My head hits the pillow, and a wave of exhaustion washes over me. Who knew someone would be tired from doing nothing all day?

With my eyes closed and the heavy blanket wrapped around me, sleep finds me quickly, dragging me into a dreamless slumber. Before my brain can shut all the way off, the sound of glass shattering rips me back to reality. My eyes blink open, and for a moment, I think maybe I've dreamt it.

Shoving into a sitting position, I toss the blanket off. I don't know how, but I instantly know something is wrong. The rational part of my brain tells me to calm down, maybe Banks just dropped a glass. But my gut tells me something else, that something terrible is about to happen. It's only a feeling, but it's strong enough to be taken seriously, very seriously.

All the exhaustion vanishes as adrenaline takes over, pumping through me with a furious fire. Holding my breath, I listen to every single noise.

When I hear the shattering of glass again, I know my gut feeling was right. Ripping the door open, I start down the hall, my feet slapping against the wood floor in a flurry.

"Stay upstairs!" Banks yells from somewhere on the first floor, clearly hearing me. "Go into your room and lock the door."

For a moment, I just stand there, my feet cemented on

the floor. I want to listen to him, I want to be safe, but how can I leave him down there all on his own. What if Xander sent more guys? What if... No, I can't think like that.

I need to... what should I do? Oh, god. I can feel the air entering my lungs, but I'm not breathing, not really. The air inside them stills. Then it hits me. I need to call the police. Patting myself down, I realize quickly that I didn't bring my phone up with me.

Shit, it's still on the kitchen table.

More glass shatters downstairs, and I find my feet moving without thought. No...wait... that wasn't downstairs. I turn around and look in the direction I think the sound came from. I think this time, it came from upstairs. Someone broke a window up here. Before I can start to move again, I see a figure appear at the end of the hallway.

Shelby.

She looks so different that I almost don't recognize her. Her normally straight, shiny hair is uncombed and messy. An unfitting gray jumpsuit is covering her slender body, and as my gaze moves down her, I notice she's not wearing any shoes. The socks on her feet are nasty, covered in dirt, and mud and have holes in them. But what makes her seem like a completely different person isn't her get up.

It's her eyes.

The look in her eyes is nothing short of bone-chilling. Cold, detached, unhinged... batshit crazy. How can this be the girl who's been my best friend all my life?

"Hello, Harlow," she greets, and even her voice sounds different, disturbing. I take a small step back, ready to make a run for the stairs to get away from her. But when she reaches around to her back and pulls out a black object from her waistband, I freeze. My heart stops. My lungs deflate. My entire life shatters.

A gun... she has a *gun*.

"Shelby, please..." I lift my hands, palms up. "Please don't do this," I beg, but she only smiles at my pleading. She smiles as if this is some kind of joke to her.

Banks must hear me, because the next thing I know, he's barreling up the stairs calling out for me.

"Don't fucking come any closer," Shelby yells. "If you do, I'll shoot her. I'll do it right now!"

I don't look back at Banks, but I can hear his footsteps falter somewhere behind me.

"Okay, okay, I won't move," Banks answers, his voice abnormally shaky. A stark contrast to his usual cocky, unfazed demeanor.

Shelby sneers, "This is all your fault, you know? Your dad and I could have been happy. I could've had it all. He loves me, and the only reason we can't be together is you." She points the gun at me as she speaks.

"What do I have to do with you and my father's relationship? If I have a say in it, I'll never see him again. You can have him."

Her pale cheeks flush with anger, "It has everything to do with you!"

"Every time I was with him, all he wanted to talk about was you. What you were doing? Who you were seeing? He was never interested in what *I* was doing. All I wanted was his attention. I wanted him to see *me*, and the only way I can have him is by getting rid of you. Then everything will be perfect." Her smile is frightening and makes the blood in my veins turn to ice.

"Please, Shelby! I'm pregnant," I sob, cradling my stomach.

"I know," she snickers. "The plan didn't go as expected." She shakes her head and points the gun at the ground.

"What do you mean?"

"How do you think you got pregnant in the first place? I exchanged your pill for placeboes. You've been taking nothing more than sugar candy," she admits, shocking the hell out of me. My mouth opens, and for once, I'm speechless. She... she did this?

"Why... why would you do that?"

Shrugging her shoulders, she says, "I thought if you got knocked up by one of the Bishops, your father would finally disown you. I guess that didn't work out. So, I'm going back to the original plan I had. It sucks a little, but killing you is all I can do now."

Shelby raises the gun again, and my mouth opens, a scream on the edge of my tongue. Then the doorbell rings. With the gun still pointed at me, she tilts her head, looking at me with shock and anger in her eyes.

"Expecting someone?"

"I-I don't know..." I really don't know. Were we expecting someone? I can't think straight with that thing pointed at me and my life on the line.

No one moves for a moment, and then the doorbell chimes once more. Then that same impatient person starts to pound on the front door, the sudden, loud noise making me jump.

"Harlow, I know you're in there. Open up!" My stepmom's muffled voice carries through the heavy front door and silent house. "I'm not leaving until you open this door and let me know that you're okay!"

Why the hell is my stepmom here?

"Well, I guess you better let her in. I can go ahead and kill two birds with one stone... Or two people with one gun," Shelby cackles.

"If you hurt her, I swear to god you'll wish you were never born," Banks threatens.

She rolls her eyes, "Go get the door, Romeo, or I'll shoot her right now, and you won't be able to do a thing to stop me."

Listening as Banks descends the stairs, I start to shake; fear and panic bubbling up.

"You don't have to do this. We've always been friends, and we still can be. Just put the gun down," I do my best to keep my voice even, but Shelby can see right through me, and instead, she takes a step closer, her eyes darkening.

"Maybe a long time ago, we were friends, but not anymore. Not ever again," tears pool in my eyes because even as crazy as Shelby is, as lost as she is, I still yearn for that person that I once knew. The person who was a friend.

I can hear someone climbing the stairs, and when I peek over my shoulder, I find my stepmother at the top of the landing. What the hell is going on? My body is caught in the crosshairs between two crazed women.

"Shelby, don't be stupid, drop the gun. Harlow, everything is going to be okay." I can hear my stepmother speaking, but I don't feel the emotion in her words. It's not going to be okay. None of this is okay.

"Me?" Shelby laughs like an evil villain, and my stepmother strolls right past me, closing in on her. "I'm not stupid. I'm not the one who doesn't even realize her husband is in love with someone else. He loves me, not you, you old hag." I can see the glint of metal peeking out of my stepmom's sleeve, the edge of it red with blood, droplets falling casually to the floor.

Slowly, I bring my hand to my mouth to stop the scream from coming out. *Banks.* Oh, god, she didn't. She wouldn't.

"Ha, then why is he with me? Why did he call the cops on you, and have you sent to a loony bin?" It's like I'm watching a nightmare play right before my eyes. I want to look away, but I can't. Shelby raises the gun to my stepmom's head, but it doesn't seem to faze her.

"Huh? It wasn't because he loves *you*?"

"Shut up!" Shelby yells her voice cracking, agony pouring out of her.

But my stepmom doesn't listen, she just continues nudging her closer and closer to the proverbial edge, "You were nothing more than convenient pussy for him. He needed you to keep an eye on Harlow and spreading your legs for him; that was just an added bonus for him."

"Stop, just stop!" Shelby screams even louder this time, the sound ringing in my ears like a siren. Lifting her hands, she presses them against her ears, and like a hawk, my eyes remain on the gun that's still in her hands. With it pointed away from us, now is our chance. Then it happens.

The moment the gun isn't pointed in my stepmom's direction anymore, she lunges for Shelby. Everything happens so fast; I can hardly make sense of it all.

A sob escapes my lips as I helplessly watch as the woman I've always known as my mother drives the already bloodied knife into Shelby's chest.

For a moment, I can't breathe, I can't move, I can't think. Time slows, and all I can do is watch Shelby die. The girl who has been my companion for most of my life stares back at me. A knife stuck in her chest, blood seeping from the wound, soaking through her gray jumpsuit. Her wide eyes bleed into mine, her face pales, and her eyes go blank.

I can see the exact moment all life leaves her. One second she is standing, the next she crumbles to the floor, landing in a heap. I don't know why, but I can't stop staring at the lifeless form on the floor. I'm unable to understand or comprehend anything that is happening. This can't be real. This has to be a dream.

A nightmare.

I know I shouldn't, but my eyes move on their own from her crumpled body, and to her eyes. I gape at the vacant look there, somehow waiting for some kind of spark to return. For her to wake up... but it's too late. She's gone, her entire life, all hopes, and dreams, every memory she ever had... gone. Just like that...

"Oh, come on. Don't act like you actually cared about her," my stepmother says nonchalantly, utterly unfazed by what she's just done.

"You-you k-killed her," I stutter. My voice coming out just as shaky as I am.

"So what? She deserved it. Truthfully, I should have killed her a long time ago," she admits. Bending down to where Shelby's body is lying on the floor, she pries the gun out of her lifeless hand. "And I should have killed you when your mother was pregnant with you. I apologize for making you go through all of this just to have it end with the same result."

Shock is all I feel. Fear. Anger. Sadness. I don't feel any of those emotions in that moment. Not like I should. It's like I'm having an out of body experience.

She killed my mother.

"Why do you look so surprised?"

Swallowing thickly, I push everything down. If I'm going to survive, I'm going to have to come up with a way to escape her.

"Why... Why did you kill her? What did she do that would make you want to kill her?"

"She took your father from me, that's what. He was always supposed to be with me. We belonged together, and she ruined it all. Just like now, how you ruined everything. I should have killed you with her, but your father and I found out early on that I couldn't have children of my own, so I thought I could raise you. I thought he would love me even more for it." A darkness overtakes her features, "I actually thought I could love you, but just like your mother, you turned out to be nothing more than an inconvenience."

An inconvenience?

The word cuts through me like a sharp knife. So many emotions flood me all at once that I can't decide which one is greater... hurt, anger, or disappointment. I'm so disappointed in myself. Disappointed that I let this woman be part of my life for so long, that I didn't see the kind of person she really was. All this time, I thought my father was the biggest monster, but as it turns out, there was a worse evil lurking.

I want to cry, to scream, to destroy the woman in front of me. I called her my mom... the woman who took my real mother from me. The walls around my fragile heart crumble as the reality of everything crashes into me.

Everything that happened, every bad thing that ever happened to me, it all boiled down to the person in front of me. It was all her fault, the rivalry, the fighting between the families, every single thing was her fault.

"I'm sorry that things have to end this way."

I don't know what compels me to do it in that moment,

but I rush her, shoving at her shoulders. A look of horror flickers in her eyes, and she stumbles backward, the gun in her hand dropping to the floor with a thud. My heart races in my chest, the sound of blood pounds in my ears, and I dart for it knowing that if I don't get it, she will. It's strictly about survival now, and if anyone is going to get out of this alive, it's going to be me.

My fingers wrap around the cold metal, and I stumble backward, nearly tripping over my feet in the process. Tremors of fear wrack my body, and my wild gaze swings to my stepmother. The weight of the gun in my hand is heavy, but it doesn't stop me from lifting it, pointing the barrel directly at her.

"You can't do it, Harlow. You aren't a killer." She taunts, and my finger shakes as I move it toward the trigger.

She's right, I'm not a killer, but when it comes to protecting my unborn baby, the men I love, and myself, I'll become anything I need to.

"Harlow, don't do something you can't live with…" Her voice trails off, and before I can even think about it, I pull the trigger. The kickback of the gun vibrates through me, and I watch completely unmoved as the bullet cuts through her chest. Her eyes go wide, and her mouth opens, but the words never come out.

A second later, she falls, just like Shelby did. My entire body clamps up, and then I start to shake watching as the only person I've had as a mother figure dies. Forcing myself to move, I drop the gun and turn running down the stairs.

Once I reach the bottom step, I yell, "Banks? Banks?"

"Over here," he weakly replies, and I rush in the direction of his voice, finding him on the ground near the door. My hands start to move, inspecting him just as my eyes are.

His hand is pressed to his side, the bright red blood seeps through his shirt, and I can barely breathe as I look into his eyes.

"Please don't die on me, Banks." Tears fall, skating down my cheeks, but I don't even feel them. All I can see is blood, it's everywhere, on my hands, on the floor. Death surrounds me, and I refuse to let it claim another person.

"Banks," I whimper, but he's slowly fading, the color draining from his face. He's lost so much blood, and there is nothing I can do.

"I love you," he says, but it sounds like a wheeze. His bright blue eyes fall closed, and panic seizes my heart.

"Don't. Stop. This isn't the end. Banks!" I scream, pressing harder against the wound. Sirens sound off in the distance, but it feels like it's too late. I can feel him leaving me.

"Please, Banks! Stay with me," I sob, but he doesn't listen. He doesn't open his eyes, and by the time the ambulance has arrived, I have no more tears to cry. In the end, my stepmother took more from me than I could have ever imagined. More than I think my heart can handle.

EPILOGUE

One Year Later

They say time heals all wounds, and I believe that. I think that as time goes on the heartache and loss, it all gets easier to deal with. The pain becomes less, the sadness isn't so suffocating, and slowly the anger toward it all fades away.

"You sure you're ready to do this?" Sullivan asks.

"Honestly, I'm not sure," I say, looking down at our four-month-old daughter. She is still so small, so fragile. Even though I know Caroline will take care of her, it's hard to let her go. Even if it's just for a few hours.

"I promise little Phoebe will be perfectly fine with me," Caroline chimes in. "We will have a great time watching classic movies, reading stories, and singing that baby shark song before bedtime."

"Oh, god, I can't hear that song anymore," Sullivan frowns.

"But, she loves it!" I interject. "And more importantly, it makes her sleepy."

"She probably wants to go to sleep to get away from that song," Sullivan grins.

"You guys just need a break, that's all. So, go, get out of the house. Go have fun. I'll send you updates every ten minutes if it will calm your mind. Just please, go do something." I know she is joking, but I actually like the ten-minute update idea. The last year has been crazy, and protecting our daughter is the most important thing to me. Since her birth, I've been with her every second of every day.

"Don't tempt her; she'll hold you to it," Oliver chuckles, walking into the living room.

"I will not," I lie, my lips pull into a sly grin.

"She will, and that's fine. Give us periodical updates. We'll be keeping Harlow busy enough to take the worry off her mind."

Caroline wrinkles her nose, "Ew, that's nasty. I don't want to hear about your sex life."

Shaking my head, I give Phoebe one last kiss before buckling her into her car seat.

You can do this. You can do this. It's just a few hours. I tell myself.

"Alright, we'll see you guys later," Caroline announces as she walks out the door, taking my entire life with her.

I watch from the window like a little kid as she puts her into the car, securing the car seat in the base.

"She's coming back, you know," Sullivan whispers into the shell of my ear, and a shiver rolls down my spine. It's insane how effortless they have to be when it comes to my body. With them, I'm in tune, every muscle, every beat of my heart, they own me, consume me. There is no them and me. Just *us* now.

"I know, but it's so hard. I've never been away from her, and all I can think about is if she's going to get enough snuggles. Is she going to miss me? What if she cries, and Caroline doesn't know what to do?" I'm rambling now, but these are all the things I worry about as a new mother.

"Let us take your mind off the small stuff for a few hours." Banks sneaks up behind me, wrapping his arms around me and pulling me back to his chest. His warmth blankets me, and I melt into his touch, letting him guide me into the bedroom. Since everything that happened, we got a new house in a new area, away from Bayshore. We wanted to a new life, a fresh start, and that meant leaving the past behind.

With both Shelby and my stepmom dead, things have finally become easier, safer, and much less complicated. But the past will always be a part of me, no matter how hard I try to forget it. It will always be there.

My father has tried to contact me a few times, but I never could bring myself to talk to him. The two people that surprisingly did stay in my life are Matt and George Bishop. I don't talk to Matt often, but we have stayed friends. We all hung out a few times, and the guys actually became friends as well. George has been telling me about my mom, my real mom. The chance to meet her was taken away from me a long time ago, but at least I have his stories to get to know her.

"What exactly are you going to do to *help* take my mind

off of things?" I smirk, knowing damn well what they all have planned. "Didn't we tell Caroline we were going out for dinner and drinks?"

Sullivan chuckles, and I can feel that deep husky sound in my bones. "Yeah, we could still do that, but we really thought about something else... something better."

"It would have been weird to tell Caroline what we really had planned," Banks points out. "Hey, Caroline, would you please watch our baby so we can have an uninterrupted fuckfest?"

Oliver punches Banks in the arm, making me giggle.

"You are such a romantic, but you do have a point," I tease, "So... what exactly do you have planned?"

"Follow us, and we'll show you," Oliver says, holding out his hand to me. I take it eagerly and let him lead me up the stairs. Banks and Sullivan follow close behind.

They lead me to my bedroom, the one I hardly ever sleep in, and Oliver motions for me to open the door. I grab the brass doorknob, turn and push the door open. When I see the inside of the room, I can't help but gasp.

The entire space is decorated beautifully. There are candles set up on the dresser and desk, illuminating the room with a dim, romantic light. Fresh cut flowers are sitting on my nightstand, giving the space a fresh, flowery scent, and rose petals are artfully laid out on the bed in a heart shape, making the whole thing just perfect.

"Oh, you guys. I love it," I say, having to hold back tears. Tears of happiness, of course. I'm just so happy and incredibly lucky. Not only did I find one man of my dreams, but I found three. Three wonderful men who love me and would do anything for me and my happiness.

We enter the room, and like always, Banks is the first one to lose his patience. I giggle as he pounces on me like a wild animal. His lips crash against mine, stealing the air from my lungs. I'm consumed by his kiss as I pull up his shirt while he undoes my pants. We only break the kiss to pull his shirt over his head. The fabric landing somewhere on the other side of the room.

As soon as Banks' upper body is free, I run my hands across his chest, stopping at the tiny raised scar where he was stabbed.

It's hard to believe that something that is so small now, barely noticeable even, almost cost him his life. I shudder just thinking about it, reliving those moments of when he was in the hospital, fighting for his life while Sullivan and Oliver promised me that everything was going to be okay. I remember falling apart, not knowing if I was ever going to come back together again.

Someone moves behind me, starting to pull up my shirt, and Banks moves from my mouth to my breasts. Pulling my bra cups down and freeing my boobs, he closes his lips around one of my nipples. My head falls back, and I moan, just as my shirt is being pulled over my head.

"You smell divine," Oliver whispers against the tender skin on my neck as he undoes my bra, letting it fall to the floor. He starts peppering open mouth kisses all along my neck, shoulders, and down my spine while his brother pays special attention to my chest.

"Lay her on the bed, so we can show her the other surprise," Sullivan urges, and the next thing I know, Banks is wrapping his arms around me, and picking me up. I throw my arms around his neck and start to giggle like a schoolgirl.

He gently deposits me on the bed and pulls my panties off in the next moment, leaving me completely naked. When I look up, I see Sullivan holding a small bottle of lotion or maybe oil, I can't really tell.

"We're going to give you a relaxing massage," Oliver grins, letting Sullivan pour some liquid into his palm.

"Yes, a very, very relaxing massage," Banks adds with a wink, while he also gets what looks to be massaging oil poured on his hands.

I smile again, but the smile turns into a low sigh when Banks' warm, oily hands land on me, slowly working into my tight muscles.

"Where did you learn to do that?" I sigh, melting into the mattress. Banks' hands move up my body, while Sullivan crawls up onto the bed and starts massaging my shoulders and neck. Oliver tends to my feet, and right then, it starts to feel like what I imagine heaven feels like.

Their big hands work my tight muscles and tender flesh until I'm nothing more than a liquid mass floating in the center of the bed.

"I hope you're ready for us," Sullivan whispers as he leans down, and nibbles on my earlobe. Banks takes that moment to suck one of my pebbled nipples into his mouth and Oliver, well, he spreads my thighs and settles between them. I can feel the heat of his breath against my core, and I shiver.

"Oh, god. It's not going to take me long with all three of you," I complain, even though it's not really a complaint. "But still, I can't get enough of you. I don't think it will ever be enough..."

"That's fine. We've got hours and days, and if that's not good enough, we've got years too." Sullivan says, sucking at my throat hard enough to leave a hickey behind. I open my mouth to speak, but the words are lost on me when I feel Oliver's rough tongue against my slit. At the same time, Banks pinches one of my nipples, and I can't help myself.

My pussy gushes and my thighs quiver with the impending pleasure that's about to be brought on me. With my clit in his mouth, Oliver enters me with two fingers, pumping in and out of me with an ounce of resistance.

"Fuck me, my cock is harder than steel right now," Banks says, his voice muffled from my breast. I try to focus on each of them individually, but I can't. The pleasure builds rising second by second, and it doesn't take me long to start going off.

"Come, baby, come all over my brother's tongue," Sullivan's filthy words only encourage me onward, and with a gasp, I lift my hips and fall apart, grinding my core into Oliver's face. Like a wild animal, he continues to feast on me, leaving not even a drop of my release behind. By the time he's done, I'm completely spent, and the brothers move away from me to slip out of their own clothing.

Watching through hooded eyes, I admire each of their bodies, my mouth watering as their rock-hard cocks come into view.

"You ready to get fucked?" Banks growls, and I nibble on my bottom lip seductively before nodding my head. He strokes his cock up and down a few times with the oil that they used on my body earlier. Then they're moving me.

Banks lifts me, and I reach out, pressing my hands down onto his impeccable chest as he impales me on his cock in one single thrust. My gaze widens, and my tongue darts out over my bottom lip. *Sweet baby Jesus.*

He stills inside of me, and I swear it's like he's grown,

gotten bigger. It doesn't hurt, but I feel fuller. Oliver appears in front of me, and Sullivan presses against my back, bending me to his will. Banks fingers dig into the flesh at my hips, holding me in place as he bucks his hips, his cock slicing me in two. At the same time, Oliver starts to stroke his cock, the mushroom tip is red and painful looking, and all I can think to do is ease his pain.

"You want my cock in your mouth?" he questions, his thick, heady voice shooting lightning bolts of pleasure through me.

"Yes," I gasp, just as Sullivan starts to lather my ass, and my puckered asshole with the oil. His fingers probe at the entrance before slipping in with ease. Slowly he fucks my ass with his fingers while Banks moves steadily in and out of me.

Like a cat in heat, I mewl, the sound radiating through Oliver's cock, which I suck on like a lollipop. Teetering back and forth between Sullivan and Banks, we slowly find a rhythm that works for all of us.

"Fuck, yes, suck me, baby. I want to come down your throat. Fill your belly with my cum." Mmm, yes. Sucking him harder, I take him deeper into my mouth, gagging when he threads his fingers through my hair and holds me against his groin. My lungs burn, and my eyes water, but as soon as he pulls back and I see the pleasure pooling in his eyes, I'm doing it all over again. With every hole filled, it doesn't take long for me to fall apart, and with my orgasm brings the brothers' orgasms.

Banks is the first to come, groaning as my clenching pussy rips every drop of sticky hot seed from his cock. Oliver is next, and I fondle his balls as he holds my head in place, fucking my throat until he finally reaches climax. I suck him off until he grows soft and slips from my mouth. Pressing a kiss to the corner of my mouth as he moves off the bed, most likely going into the bathroom.

With two out of the three done, I push back against Sullivan, and he meets my thrust, slamming into me with the same intense need. His touch is rough, and all I can feel is his cock taking my ass.

"Please fill my ass with your cum," I whimper, knowing how he loves it when I talk dirty. Peering at him over my shoulder, we lock eyes, and his thrusts become harder, almost painful, but like a volcanic eruption, I feel my own climax sneaking up on me. Thrust. Thrust. The sound of our skin slapping fills the room, and my mouth pops open, a delightful moan escaping.

Banks smirks at me, and I can feel the bite of pain as he rolls my hardened nipples between two fingers.

"Come on, baby, you can come again. I know you can..." Banks encourages, the look in his eyes is dark, heated, and like waves cresting the beach, my orgasm slams into me. At the same time, a roar that could wake the dead pierces the air. Sagging against Banks' sweaty body, I smile floating down from my own orgasm while Sullivan fills me with every drop of his release.

My lids start to grow heavy immediately after. It's been a long time since we did a threesome, and with a baby, there isn't much time for sex, let alone with all three of them.

"You okay?" Sullivan asks, his fingers caressing my back.

"More than okay. I'm pretty sure I've become a pile of liquid mush."

"No worries, we'll let you sleep for a little while before we go for round two."

That causes me to perk up, "Round two?" I roll off Banks, and sit up on the bed, my eyes moving between all three of the men I love.

"Yes, round two, and three, and four, and..."

Oliver rolls his eyes, "I think she gets it. We want to fuck her."

"Oh, that's not the only thing we want," Banks snickers and jumps off the bed. Confusion isn't even a word I would use to describe how I'm feeling, still my brow furrows, and I try and comprehend what is happening.

"What do you mean?" I direct my question to all three of them.

"We started as enemies," Oliver says.

"We became lovers," Sullivan says next.

"We have saved each other, and had a baby," Banks adds.

"And?" I say, my heart beating out of my chest.

The brothers look to each other before Sullivan pulls out a black velvet box. It's then that I know what is happening.

"Will you do us the honor of becoming Mrs. Bishop?"

What? How? What do I even say to that? After all we've gone through? After everything that's happened, there is no way I could ever say no.

We're more than just fated rivals.

We're lovers, we're a family, and together we beat the odds. We got our happily ever after, and so much more.

"Of fucking course. I'd love nothing more than to be tied to the three men I love for life."

Something that resembles relief appears on each of their faces, and within seconds the heavy, three stone diamond ring is placed on my finger. Nestled between the three diamonds is one smaller one, and I know right away the symbolism of that ring. It was designed with a purpose. Our story.

 Three Brothers.
 One love story.
 A lifetime of love.

The End

ALSO BY THE AUTHORS

CONTEMPORAY ROMANCE

The Bet
The Dare
The Secret
The Vow

Also by the Authors

Kiss Me Never

Bayshore Rivals
(Reverse Harem Bully Romance)

When Rivals Fall
When Rivals Lose
When Rivals Love

***

DARK ROMANCE

The Rossi Crime Family
(Dark Mafia Romance)

Convict Me
Protect Me
Keep Me
Guard Me
Tame Me
Remember Me

Hating You
(Bully Romance)

***

EROTIC STANDALONES

Also by the Authors

Runaway Bride
FREE NOVELLA

There Captive
(A Dark Reverse Harem)

Beck and Hallman
BLEEDING HEART ROMANCE

- [f] CASSANDRAHALLMAN
  AUTHORJLBECK
- [IG] CASSANDRA_HALLMAN
  AUTHORJLBECK
- [BB] CASSANDRAHALLMAN
  JLBECK

Printed in Great
Britain
by Amazon